Unintentional

M.E. Clayton

DEDICATION

For anyone who has ever wanted to find their way back..

CONTENTS

ACKNOWLEDGMENTS

The first acknowledgment will always be my husband. There aren't enough words to express my gratitude for having this man in my life. There is a little bit of him in every hero I dream up, and I can't thank God enough for bringing him into my life. Thirty years, and still going strong!

Second, there's my family; my daughter, my son, my grandchildren, my sister, and my mother. Family is everything, and I have one of the best. They are truly the best cheerleaders I could ever ask for, and I never forget just how truly blessed I am to have them in my life.

And, of course, there's Kamala. This woman is not only my beta and idea guinea pig, but she's also one of my closest friends. She's been with me from the beginning of this journey, and we're going to ride this thing to the end. Kam's the encouragement that sparked it all, folks.

And, finally, I'd like to thank everyone who's purchased, read, reviewed, shared, and supported me and my writing. Thank you so much for helping make this dream a reality and a happy, fun one at that! I cannot say thank you enough.

PROLOGUE

Falling in love is easy. Probably because most of the time you're actually falling into the idea of love and not actual love itself. Staying in love? Now, that's the hard part.

There are thousands and thousands of people walking the planet who are in love with love.

You know, the feeling of novelty. The giddiness when you receive flowers or candy. The butterflies you get when you see their name flash across your smart phone screen.

Yeah.

That bullshit.

So, how can you tell if you're in love with love or in love with the actual person? It's easy. Pay attention to how you feel when the shine wears off.

That first time you walk into the bathroom and his underwear is lying on the floor *next* to the hamper instead of in it? The first time she doesn't shave her legs for you? The first time someone has a horrible stomachache, and you just *know* what they're doing inside the bathroom? Pay attention to how you feel when that shit is going down and that will tell you a lot. Do you feel annoyed or irritated? There is a difference, you see.

If you're merely annoyed, you'll mention it the next time you see him/her and remind them that you're their wife/husband and not their mother/father, so they need to pick up after themselves.

If you're irritated, you'll probably let it fester until you can't hold it in any longer, then finally spew out all kinds of vile shit that you can't take back, and then there goes that.

Irritation is the shine wearing off, folks.

Once you're irritated, everything that person doesn't do perfectly will begin to irritate you. That's when other people who show you any ounce of attention start looking mighty shiny.

Real relationships are not all unicorns, fairy dust, and sexual bliss. It doesn't matter if you have twenty kids, no kids, or one kid and a goldfish because *life happens*.

You get comfortable. You get sloppy. You get content. You get complacent.

You fall prey to the 'oh, that's just marriage' hype.

Fuck. That. Shit.

Your marriage is what you make it, and most people make it predictable. And once your marriage falls into predictability, husband and wife run the risk of turning into roommates, forgetting all about how they used to be lovers.

That's a dangerous place to be in your marriage.

Life has a magical, devious, unsuspecting way of turning husbands into fathers, workaholics, and financial stressors. It turns wives into mothers, homemakers, and tired family organizers. We forget that we're still supposed to be husbands and wives to one another. We forget we're supposed to be in love.

You have to pay attention, folks.

Pay attention to the first time your wife tells you she's too tired for sex. Pay attention to the first time your husband tells you he's working late. Pay attention to the first time an anniversary is forgotten or the first time neither one of you cares about Valentine's Day or your anniversary.

However, pay *special* attention to the first time your husband tells you he's going to the gym when he's never been before. Pay *special* attention to the first time your wife comes home with new lingerie when she's never worn it before.

See, this is where we're bass-ackward. We get married, and within the first five years, we start gaining weight, or stop doing our hair, or quit dressing up, or quit buying flowers, etc. However, the minute we file for divorce, we're at the gym losing weight, or at the salon getting our hair done, or at the mall buying new tailored suits.

We're perfectly okay with looking our worst for the person we love, but we go out of our way to look our best for people we don't even know.

What the fuck is that nonsense?

Shouldn't our spouses get the best of everything we have? If you pledge your *life* to someone, aren't they worth putting on a little lipstick for? Opening the door for? *Something?*

Well, my marriage found its way into the roommate stage, and I was actually fine with it until it was horrifically brought to my attention that I no longer satisfied my wife in bed.

Women's what-the-fuck moment is when their husbands quit making them feel beautiful and loved. Men's what-the-fuck moment is when their wives are no longer screaming out their names during sex.

When I hit my what-the-fuck moment, I realized how much I missed my wife and how much I needed to get her back. Mostly, I realized just how much of an idiot I'd been.

Here's the sad story of how completely lost I was and how I had taken my wife with me.

CHAPTER 1

Marcus ~

"Holy crap." I thought I heard Cynthia exclaim through the open window that faced out towards the patio. "I can't believe you let him do that to you." It was Friday night and my wife's monthly girls' night with her college friends.

I could hear Teri's answer clearly. "At this point, I'd let that man do whatever the hell he wants to me. Sex with him is *that* good."

Their monthly girls' night was on a house rotation, and this month, it ended up being at our house. I've always made myself scarce when it was my wife's turn, and usually, everyone was gone by the time I got home, but I guess not tonight. I knew I shouldn't be listening in, but a man could learn a lot from unguarded, drunk, strong women. Especially, from Teri. That woman was as unguarded sober as she was drunk.

Teri, Cynthia, and Jackie were Emily's best friends, and they have been since college. Teri Struster was the advertisement executive who opted for the single life and had no children. Cynthia Elgin was a high school economics teacher who married her high school sweetheart and had twin boys. Jackie Artley was a law office assistant who was remarried and had a blended household of a daughter and stepdaughter.

With the fact that we were all reaching our forties in a couple of years, it was amazing to me that my wife and her friends had managed to remain so close throughout all these years. Their girls' night out was something I never begrudged her because loyal, lifelong friends were rare, indeed. Plus, I loved seeing Emily happy.

"That must mean he's hung like a horse," Cynthia suggested.

"Nope," Teri replied, popping her 'p'. "He's your average white male in all those statistical studies. He's has a respectable six inches or so."

"Wait, wait, wait." I could hear Jackie join in. "He's only packing six inches, but he's damn near the best sex you've ever had?"

I knew I shouldn't be listening, and I was, honest-to-God, going to retreat to the privacy of the bedroom, but when Emily spoke, my wife's voice pulled at my curiosity and my feet remained planted in the kitchen.

"Yeah, you need to explain that phenomenon to me. You've been with some of the hottest men I've ever seen that have packed way more. Please explain, ma'am," Emily instructed.

"He's that book boyfriend come to life, ladies," Teri explained. "You know all that crap about a man wanting you so badly that he tears your panties off with his teeth? Or how he fucks you in a dirty alley behind a restaurant because he wants you so badly that he can't wait until you find a respectable bedroom?"

"Yeah," Emily replied. "The whole he-makes-you-feel-like-you're-the-only-woman-on-the-planet sort of heat."

"Well, that's how Christopher makes me feel and it's addicting as hell," Teri continued. "He does the entire dance, ladies. From the tearing off my clothes to going down on me for hours to leaving his mark all over my body to just…" She let out an appreciative sigh. "He makes me feel like I'm the most beautiful woman he's ever been with. And even if it's not true, I feel like it is, and I'll keep letting him do whatever the hell he wants to me if he keeps making me feel like that."

"Well, goddamn," Jackie muttered.

"Well, Emily knows what I mean. Right, Em?"

"Me? What do you mean, *me?"*

My entire body froze at the sound of her incredulousness.

"Oh, c'mon, Em," Teri drawled out. "Even knocking on forty's door, Marcus is still hot as hell, and you guys have no children to distract you from one another. You can't tell me that he doesn't come home all sweating and dirty from the construction site and just fucks you all over the house until you're a blubbering idiot?"

I could hear Emily choking on her wine accompanied by a whacking sound. "Jesus, Em, you okay?" Cynthia asked.

"I…I…I'm f…fine," she rasped out.

"Well?" Teri prodded.

"Well, what?" my wife asked once she got herself under control.

"You're telling me that you and Marcus don't go at it like rabbits anymore?" I should have been upset at the obvious invasion of privacy into our sex life, but I wasn't. I wasn't naïve enough to believe that women weren't just as candid about sex as men were. In all actuality, I was waiting on Emily's answer just as badly as the girls were.

"First of all, Marcus doesn't come home dirty often anymore," Emily began. "Being the owner of the company doesn't allow for him to be on the construction sites all that much. That's what he has supervisors and foremen for. Secondly, just because we decided not to have children that doesn't mean our careers aren't demanding and time consuming." I heard her pause. I assumed she was taking a drink of her wine. "We go to bed tired just like couples with children, too, you know."

"Wait, wait, wait. Are you telling us that marital sex turns into missionary with your socks on *even* if you don't have children?" Jackie asked incredulously.

"No," Emily answered. "What I'm saying is that, even without children, sex can take a backseat to real life."

"That's fucking depressing," Teri grumbled.

"No, it's not," Emily denied. "Just because Marcus isn't tearing off my panties with his teeth that doesn't mean our sex life isn't good. We're fine."

Fine?

Our sex life was *fine?*

Look, I couldn't care less how long a man's been in his relationship, no man wanted to hear his wife or girlfriend describe their sex life as fucking *fine*. It might be macho bullshit, but…

There was a heartbeat of silence before Cynthia broke it. "Okay, can we ditch the boring marital sex and get back to how Christopher makes your toes curl? I mean, no offense, but if I want to hear about married sex, I'll replay how Martin and I eked out five minutes of sexual bliss last week before the twins woke up. I want to hear about Christopher and all his magical six inches."

I could hear all the girls laugh. "He just *knows*," Teri continued. "While I think we're all still fabulous at our ages, it's no secret that women tend to become more insecure with age." I could hear a bunch of murmurs in agreement. "Wrinkles start to appear, skin starts to sag, weight is harder to fight off, and then it seems like everywhere you look, younger, hotter, perkier females are everywhere. Well, Christopher makes me feel like I've been dipped in the fountain of youth. He just gets women, and if I weren't still riding the high from his touch, I'd recommend he hire himself out and bring smiles to women all over the world. Like a public service."

"I'm lucky if Martin stops me from leaving the house with cheesy macaroni in my hair. You can forget about him telling me I'm pretty or look nice," Cynthia laughed.

Jackie laughed, too. "I hear you. Jackson and I aren't any different. We get into bed, and I swear to God, we'll look over at each other and ask the other if they want to have sex, and three out of five times the answer is no."

I could hear Emily laugh lightly at the accounts of their sex lives. It wasn't until she spoke that I felt my stomach drop. "Yes, can we get back to Christopher, please?"

It took amazing personal restraint not to lose my shit at Emily's request to hear more about another man. Back to no man wanting to hear his wife or girlfriend describe their sex life as fine…well, no man definitely wanted to hear his wife or girlfriend beg for details about another man.

Who was apparently a sex god, no less.

I personally didn't want to hear any more about Christopher, so I did the unthinkable.

I purposely put an end to their girls' night.

I walked out onto the patio, making my presence known. "Ladies," I greeted, and four female heads swiveled my way.

"Hey, Marcus," Cynthia greeted.

"Hi, Marcus," Jackie replied, smiling.

"Hey," Teri saluted, short and sweet.

"Marcus," Emily acknowledged, then looked at the watch that adorned her wrist. "Oh, wow. I didn't realize it was so late." She grimaced a bit. "Sorry."

I shook my head as I walked over. "No need to be sorry." The girls were all sitting in our deck chairs that surrounded a fire pit, but as it was April, there was no fire lit. I leaned down and kissed Emily on the top of her head, ignoring her rounded and blinking eyes. "I'm going to head on inside. You girls go on and keep having fun." I noted four pairs of eyes ranging from brown, blue, and green darting around, clearly realizing they couldn't continue with their praises of the magically gifted Christopher.

"Uh, no...no," Teri objected. "It's about that time we all head out anyway."

"Uh, yeah...the kids get up early and all that..." Jackie joined in.

Cynthia stood up and gave me a sheepish head nod. "It is kind of late and who knows what kind of chaos is happening at home without us."

Emily stood and it didn't sit well with me that she still had a confused look on her face. "Uh, it's fine. We..." She studied my face a second longer. "Are you okay?"

I looked at my beautiful wife and I wanted to kick my own ass. She wanted to know if something was wrong with me because I kissed the top of her head. Could I be any more of a jackass?

Seriously? Could I?

I just smiled back at her. "I'm fine, Chill." I had nicknamed her Chill back in college because she used to get so stressed-out during finals that I sometimes feared she'd have a damn panic attack.

She didn't look convinced. "Let me walk the girls out and-"

"Pfft, you don't need to walk us out, Em." Jackie flapped a hand at her. "We all know our own way out." Cynthia stood up as Jackie and Teri did.

"Do you want help with all this," Teri asked, making a gesture towards all the bottles and glasses out on the patio drink trays.

I answered before Emily could. "That's okay, Teri. I'll help Emily clean up."

She nodded and I stepped back as all the women stopped to give Emily a hug on their way out. I was lucky in the respect that I genuinely liked all my wife's friends. They were all very different from each other, but their loyalty turned those differences into strengths. Each woman on her own was beautiful, strong, and successful. However, put them together and they could probably impeach The President.

Emily started gathering up the glasses, so I followed suit and picked up the empty wine bottles, then following her into the kitchen. We made a second trip, and I dumped all the bottles in our recycle bin as Emily started washing the glasses.

I eyed her as she stood in front of the sink and decided to test her earlier reaction to my kiss. I wasn't quick tempered, that would be my brother, Matthew. I had been blessed with the ability to assess a situation before I reacted. I could probably count on one hand how many times in my life I've flown off the handle and they'd all been with good reason. My mother would often joke that if I snapped, the person on the receiving end completely deserved it.

Cleaning the patio gave me time to realize that I was probably reading too much into the pieces of conversation I'd overheard. Maybe the only reason Emily used the word fine to describe our sex life was because she didn't feel comfortable giving out details, thinking it might make me uncomfortable. I mean, that's a completely logical assessment of the comment, right?

I walked up behind my wife, and wrapping my arms around her waist, rested my chin on her head. Emily was only five-foot-three to my six-foot-two, so I always towered over her, and I secretly loved that.

What I didn't love was how her entire body tensed up as my arms went around her. "Marcus, what are you doing?"

I tightened my jaw and tried to control the tenor of my voice. Remember, I was the rational situation assessing one. "I'm hugging my wife."

She let a heartbeat of silence go by before adding, "I gathered that much. I guess, what I should have asked was *why?*"

I released her and took a step back as she turned around to face me. If I thought she looked confused earlier on the patio, that was nothing compared to the look of actual worry on her face now. "I can't hug my wife?"

Her perfectly arched brows shot up. "You *can*, but you just never do…so, I'm just kind of wondering what's going on. Are you sure you're okay, Marcus?"

"That's bullshit, Chill. I hug you all the time," I argued.

Her brow furrowed and she crossed her arms over her chest as she regarded me. "When?"

"What?"

She leaned forward a bit. *"When?* When do you ever hug me just to hug me?"

I stood there and prayed that The Lord would flood my mind with memories of me randomly hugging her, but The Lord was clearly trying to teach me a lesson because nothing was coming to mind.

Nothing.

Emily stood there patiently until she smirked, realizing she was the undeniable victor this round. "Fine, Chill," I conceded. "Still, it doesn't mean

I can't hug you if I feel the desire to."

Her head tilted a bit and she gifted me with one of her brilliant smiles. "Of course, it doesn't, Marcus. But that doesn't mean I'm not going to ask you if you're okay when you act out of character." She walked up to me, then kissed my cheek. "I'm going to go shower."

Emily left me standing alone in our kitchen as her words played over and over in my head. Hugging her and kissing her was me acting *out* of character?

Fuck.

CHAPTER 2

Emily ~

I stood under the hot water, letting the spray beat on my shoulder muscles, and it felt glorious.

Our remodeled bathroom was one of the few luxurious indulgences Marcus and I had treated ourselves to when his construction company had finally started making a respectable profit. We had never moved on or moved up from our typical four-bedroom, two-bath suburbia home because neither of us had seen the need.

Marcus and I had met in our senior year of college at the ripe old age of twenty-two, and while it hadn't been a love at first sight situation, it had turned into love, and we had gotten married five years later. After we'd graduated from college, Marcus had worked in construction for about five years, and when he had felt that he'd learned enough about construction from the ground up, he had finally put his degree in structural engineering to use and had started up his own construction company. The first five years had been exciting, scary, thrilling, and terrifying all at the same time. However, the next five had proven successful, and now Maxwell Construction was a respectable name in the industry.

I had graduated with a degree in business management, but my aspirations hadn't been as exciting as Marcus'. I had gone out into the world, certain that my degree was going to hand me my dream job, but sadly, it hadn't. I had worked a handful of different jobs before I had landed a position with Swan Interior Designs. I worked as Melissa Swan's executive assistant, and I couldn't be happier.

Melissa didn't treat me as a lowly assistant. She actually treated me as if I were her equal partner. She asked my opinions and discussed company business with me, making me feel as if she truly valued me. Some might say that I wasted my degree by stopping at the level of someone's assistant, but I was happy. Plus, I'd rather be happy with a mediocre job title than be the vice president of senior sales-or some such nonsense-and be miserable.

In my quest to find myself and Marcus' quest to start his own company, we had never gotten around to having children. However, I'd never been one of those women whose life plan had to include children. I liked them, but they weren't necessary to make my life feel complete, and Marcus was of the same mind. Also, I think the fact that his brother, Matthew, had three children helped. Whenever we were in need of some minor-aged company, we'd pick up Matt's kids for the weekend.

So, since it was just Marcus and I, the house we lived in since we got married still worked well for us all these years later. We weren't the flashy type, so our home and cars didn't need to reflect what was in our bank accounts. Besides, I secretly loved that Cynthia and Jackie were a few streets over from us and we could visit often. Teri was the only one who chose to live directly in the city, but it worked for her single lifestyle.

I heard the door to the bathroom open and knew Marcus was starting his nighttime ritual of brushing his teeth, then undressing, throwing his clothes in the hamper. We had a quiet routine that worked for the both of us. We were never in each other's way, and with the remodel of the bathroom, we had enough room to do what we each needed to do without stepping over each other.

I had my eyes closed, enjoying the jet streams, when I heard the shower door open. What could possibly be so important that Marcus needed to interrupt my shower? I straightened my back, opened my eyes, then looked over at him.

Surprisingly, Marcus was naked and coming into the shower with me.

Why in the hell was he naked? And why was he showering with me?

"What are you doing?" I asked as I blinked water out of my eyes.

His entire body froze as he was halfway into the shower. He blinked twice and I stepped back as he took a deep breath.

What the hell was going on?

"I thought I'd take a quick shower with you," he explained as his body moved again, shutting the shower door behind him.

I wasn't sure what the expression on my face was, but if Marcus' expression was any indication, I wasn't wearing a happy-to-see-you face. In thinking about it, I should be happy that my husband wanted to shower with me, right? Still, even though I *wanted* to be happy that my husband wanted to shower with me, he hasn't joined me for a shower in *years*. Between the kiss and hug earlier, and now this, I was starting to worry a bit. "Why?"

His jaw clenched as he reached over my head to grab the soap. "Is joining you in the shower a problem for you?"

I stepped back and looked up at him a little stunned. "No. Of course, it isn't. I just…you normally don't, so I was just asking."

He lathered up and started washing his body, and to say the silence was awkward was a super understatement. My relaxing shower had suddenly turned into a rush to finish the minimum and get the hell out of here.

I was just reaching for my shampoo when a strong, wet, soapy, masculine arm beat me to it. I wanted to ask him why he grabbed my shampoo, but with his previous reactions to my questions tonight, I decided against it. I figured if he wanted his hair to smell like Strawberry Swiss, who was I to criticize? It wasn't until he put the bottle back and I felt his hands in my hair that I realized he wasn't going for the Strawberry Swiss smell at all.

Marcus was washing my freakin' hair.

I had no idea what to make of that.

I wanted to ask what the hell was going on with him so badly, but I didn't for two reasons. First, he hasn't seemed partial to any of my questions so far. Secondly, it felt so good to have him wash my hair that I actually moaned.

"Does that feel good?"

I didn't speak, but just nodded my head and closed my eyes again. I wanted to get lost in the sensations he was lavishing on me, but it was hard to squelch all the questions in my head. Marcus and I stopped doing the romance and affection bit a long time ago. I knew I wasn't Marcus' ideal woman, and while that fact should probably bother me, it didn't. I didn't mind where his fantasies lay as long as he was kind and remained faithful to his vows. I knew he cared about me and that was enough.

A lot of women would accuse me of selling myself short or settling, but even though I wasn't Marcus' ideal woman, he was my ideal man. I loved my husband and he treated me well. I was pretty okay with that.

My musings were interrupted when I felt Marcus grab my shoulders and turn me around. I instinctively tilted my head back to rinse the shampoo out of my hair, but that simple act turned into an embarrassingly unexpected scene.

I had my eyes closed and head tilted back when I felt Marcus' hands on my hips and his lips on my stomach. I was so startled, I opened my eyes-yes, I opened my eyes as I was rinsing *shampoo* out of my hair-and as soon as the suds hit my eyes, I started jumping around, smacking Marcus in the forehead, and causing him to fall back on his ass.

"What the hell, Chill?"

I turned around and stuck my face under the water, then opening and closing my eyes to try to alleviate the burning. My eyes felt like they were on fire, so Marcus was on his own.

The pain in my eyes was finally starting to ease when I heard the shower door open, then I think slam shut. I wasn't sure because…well, my eyes were on goddamn fire. It took a couple of minutes, but I was finally able to open them without praying for death and, yep, I was once again alone in the shower.

I quickly finished up my shower and actually felt sad that my previous planned relaxing shower had turned out to be a session of surprise and torture.

What the hell had Marcus been trying to do?

He never went down on me anymore, so why in the hell would he have his lips all over my stomach? Was he just trying to be affectionate again, like the kiss on the patio and the hug in the kitchen? I mean, seriously, *what the hell?*

Plus, if he was just trying to be affectionate, why was he kissing me so close to my lady place? It's been eons since Marcus and I have had any foreplay in our sex life, so why now?

I meant what I had told the girls earlier tonight. My sex life with Marcus was fine. Sure, it lacked that all-consuming passion, but the fact that Marcus had a big dick more than made up for it. In comparison to the two sexual partners that had come before him, Marcus was packing some serious weight in the penis department.

I knew I was biased, but Teri was right when she had said Marcus was still hot as hell. Marcus was six-foot-two-inches with raven black hair and grey eyes that could look right through you. His brows match his hair and those grey orbs of his were surrounded by eyelashes that women spend hundreds to have. His face was made up of sharp, masculine angles, and his lips were full and soft when he wanted them to be.

His face was masculine perfection, but the faint scar that ran down from his right eyebrow to his cheekbone and the scar that sexily marred the right side of his upper lip gave him a hot quality that you only read about in romance novels. He had been fourteen when he had ridden into a fence on his bike and the collision had caused his face to scrape down a broken wooden plank. Of course, at the time it had been horrific, but the scars that remained added to his beauty. He also had a set of dimples that…well, dimples, enough said.

His body was another thing of appreciation.

Some of it was diligence and hard work while the rest was just good genes. His father was sixty-three-years-old, and he still had decent muscle mass without being overweight. The fact that Marcus worked in construction attributed a lot to his hard body. He exercised when he could, but it didn't seem necessary since, at thirty-eight-years-old, that man still had a six pack you could cut diamonds on. He had a wide chest and big, muscular arms. His waist tapered into a hip area that you couldn't help but want to lick. And the rest of him was made up of powerful, muscular legs. If that wasn't enough, the man also had tattoos.

I knew he was my husband, but the man was scorching hot.

And since he was hot and packing a big dick, sex with Marcus was never bad. Sure, foreplay was nonexistent, and we may not kiss a lot or touch, but the sex was still great. Once he got inside me, nothing else mattered. He had no problem making me cum, and when he didn't, it was because I was inside my own head, and I wasn't connecting.

I didn't mind the lack of kissing and touching because, again, Marcus treated me kindly and my life was too blessed to complain or throw pity parties because it wasn't perfect. My life was great by a lot of people's standards and that's what I tried to focus on.

I knew I was the reason that we've lost touch of the romantic side of our marriage, but Marcus has never complained or commented, so as far as I was concerned, our marriage was fine the way it was. So, why was he all of a sudden wanting to be…be *loving?*

I quickly brushed my hair out, then threw it into a wet, messy bun on top of my head. I brushed my teeth, then wrapping myself up in my bathrobe, decided to ask Marcus what was going on.

A woman's mind was a terrible, dangerous place. If left on its own, it had the ability to conjure up the very worst of scenarios until you were paralyzed by the paranoia of self-doubt and insecurity.

Like, right now. Normality was safe. It was easy and it was reassuring. If nothing was wrong, it was safe to say that nothing will continue to be wrong because nothing out of the norm was happening. Well, Marcus kissing, hugging, and touching me was out of the norm. So, while I was trying to remain calm and I was trying-*I swear I was*-to just appreciate the attention and affection, I was really freaking the hell out.

I walked out of the bathroom and found Marcus dressed in a pair of low-riding pajama pants only. He stood near the bed, barefoot and shirtless, and the sight of him still had the power to make my heart lurch unexpectedly. The tattoos that covered the right side of his chest to his arm were front and center.

He was so damn handsome.

I wasn't an ugly duckling, but I still reveled in the incredibility that he was my husband. This gorgeous, generous, and at the moment, irritated man was *my* husband.

He watched silently as I walked farther into the room. I knew he was upset, but it wasn't like I had planned on whacking him in the head and knocking him on his ass in the shower.

"Are you okay? I'm sorry about knocking you over," I apologized. Even though I didn't think I was to blame for his foul mood, I didn't want to go to sleep uneasy over the shower debacle.

Marcus crossed his arms over his hard chest and took in a deep breath before answering me. "Why do you tense up every time I touch you?"

What? "I don't-"

He held up a hand to stop my automatic denial. "Yes, you do."

"Marcus-" I tried again.

"Look, I realized that we don't…I know we're not the most affectionate couple around, but that isn't a good enough excuse for why you'd flinch uncomfortably from my touch. I'm your goddamn husband, and whether I touch you every day or once every five years, it shouldn't make you wary and uncomfortable, Emily."

I was starting to get irritated my-damn-self. I understood what he was asking, but he was behaving as if my wariness was out of line. It wasn't. Anyone would question it if, all of a sudden, their spouse started lavishing them with attention when it's been years since they've been affectionate with you. It wasn't that I was opposed to being loving and demonstrative, I had just been surprised, and he couldn't get mad at me for that.

Apparently, he wasn't done being the victim, though. "Is there a reason my touch makes you uncomfortable?"

I planted my hands on my hips. "Is there a reason that, why after over what has to be at least a couple of years, you all of a sudden *want* to touch me?" I countered.

"You're my fucking wife, Emily. What do you except me to do if I can't touch you without you flinching or questioning my intent?"

What's he supposed to do if he doesn't feel comfortable touching me?

So, if he wasn't free or comfortable to touch me…

I swear, in my head, my next words made total sense. *"Are you cheating on me?"*

CHAPTER 3

Marcus ~

I've never laid a hand on my wife out of anger, but the fact that she could even ask me that question had my blood boiling and my vision red. "Are you out of your *fucking* mind?" I seethed. "Did you really just ask me if I'm fucking *cheating* on you?"

Emily threw her arms up in a frustrated fashion. "What else am I supposed to think when you come home all of a sudden wanting to be in love with me, then imply that what choice do you have if you can't touch me?"

"You can think whatever the fuck you want, Emily! But you're not supposed to automatically conclude that I'm fucking someone else!" I roared.

"Then what the hell is all this about, Marcus?" Emily's temper was coming out and I knew this was going to go all bad. "You never kiss or hug me, and you know it! But you dare to stand there, acting offended, because I'm confused by your sudden behavior?"

"Maybe I miss kissing you and touching you. Did you ever think about that?" I countered. "Instead, it makes more sense to you that I must be cheating on you and not that I just missing holding you? And as for suddenly wanting to be in love with you, I have news for you, Emily, I *am* in love with you. There's no *suddenly* about it." I uncrossed my arms and started pacing the bedroom.

I was pissed.

So fucking pissed, and not necessarily at my wife, either.

I was pissed that I let our marriage get to a point where I stopped touching my wife to the point where she felt uncomfortable when I did. After a couple of years, the first effort at affection ends with her accusing me of cheating on her.

What in the ever-lovin' fuck?

I stopped my pacing and went to stand in front of her. "Look at me, Emily." She lifted her head and I almost stepped back. I wasn't expecting her

16

beautiful green eyes to be swirling in so much anger and resentment. "What have I ever done that would make you think I would *ever* cheat on you?" Her eyes couldn't hold my gaze, and when they started darting all over the room instead of focusing on me, I knew this was going to be bad. "Emily?"

I could see her chest move with the deep breath that she took in, then released. "Marcus, let's not do this. We-"

"Not do what?" I interrupted.

I did end up stepping back when her eyes found mine again and they were swimming in unshed tears. "Don't make me say it, Marcus. Once I tell you, I can't take the words back," she replied quietly. "They're going to exist between us and…I like our life the way it is. I'm happy with you as we are."

Now I *needed* to know the source of her assumption, and this night wasn't coming to an end until she told me everything. "So help me God, Emily, if you've-"

She grabbed at my arms. "No! God, Marcus, no! There's no one else, I swear."

"Then what the fuck is going on?"

I watched her as she let go of my arms, walked over to the bed, dropped down, then sat with her hands in her lap. She looked up at me as she came clean about her feelings. "Do you remember a couple of years ago when Scott Holden stopped by on his way to Oregon and you guys spent the night outside drinking and reminiscing?"

I nodded. "Of course, I remember." We had gotten so drunk that night that my hangover had lasted almost two goddamn days. I haven't had alcohol like that since that night. I'd never been so drunk, and the memory still made me a tad queasy.

Emily started gnawing on the corner of her lower lip. A tear slipped out and she wiped it away so quickly that it was as if she hadn't wanted it to exist. "I had woken up thirsty shortly after I had gone to sleep, so I…" She took another deep breath. "I went to the kitchen to get a glass of water and your voices carried through the open window into the kitchen. I…uh, heard some of your conversation."

I stilled. I tried running that night through my mind, but I had been so drunk that I had lost most of that night the very next morning when I had awoken. We had talked about old times and new times and just standard bullshit. I had no idea what she could have overheard that would make her think I was capable of cheating on her.

I walked over to the cushioned armchair in the corner of our bedroom and sat down with my elbows resting on my knees and my hands clamped together. "Emily, I was so drunk that night, I couldn't tell you much of what me and Scott talked about."

She nodded in these sad jerking motions and my heart started to actually hurt. "I don't know what all you guys were talking about, but I walked in to hearing you…" She had to clear her throat before continuing. "Uh, you were telling Scott that...that there was only one woman that you've ever been with that you'd been sex-crazed for."

What?

No.

Fuck.

"You were telling him how Stacy Spencer had turned you on so much to the point that you'd...uh, you'd eat her pussy, even if she hadn't showered for a week." Emily's spine straightened and I could see her doing her best to be strong despite the tears that were now quietly running down her face. "Scott joked that he loved women so much that there's nothing he wouldn't do whether a woman had showered or not."

"Emily-"

Her eyes fired at me. "No, Marcus. You're the one who insisted on having this conversation," she reminded me, "so we're going to have it." She swiped at her face again, but the tears just kept on flowing. "You responded to Scott's joking by explaining how not you. That...that with the *exception of Stacy*, you prefer your women clean before you kiss or touch them. How you're not a fan of salty sweat or the taste of lotions or perfumes and stuff."

"Emily, you're my *wife*. You can't believe-"

Emily went on as if I hadn't spoken. "I couldn't stand to hear any more, so I turned to leave, but then...then Scott asked how you ended up with me if you were so crazed for Stacy." She let out a pathetic huff of a laugh, like reacting to a bad joke. "God, help me, I stayed around to hear your answer. I shouldn't have, and I guess that's what I get for eavesdropping, but I can't change that now. You told him Stacy had to finally submit to her father's wishes and marry some family friend who had money and she had to quit screwing around. You met me six months later and that was that."

I felt like my heart was going to break through my ribs and bleed out at her feet. I'd like to say that I was so drunk that my actions and words should be excused, but drunk or not, I knew better. The only woman I should ever praise or discuss in such a reverent manner was my wife. "Emily-"

She held her hand up in a halting motion. "I'd never condemn you for being honest, Marcus. I shouldn't have eavesdropped, and I accept that. I also spent the following days weighing my life against your words, and the fact of the matter was that my life was good-it *is* good. I might be second choice to Stacy, but you've always been kind to me and a good provider. The big picture of my life is great, and I made a conscious choice to accept my place with you and be okay with it."

I started shaking. "But you're not my second choice, Em-"

Again, she went on as if I hadn't spoken. "It's the intimacy that was a little harder to work through. After that night, every time you touched me, all I could think about was how clean I was. I wondered if my perfume was too strong or how long it'd been since I showered. I'd replay the day to recall if I...uh, sweated. You know, ridiculous crap like that."

She was fucking breaking my heart.

"Emily, stop-"

She narrowed her eyes at me. "So, it's okay to talk about how I make you feel when I flinch from your touch, but it's not okay to talk about how you make me feel when you touch me?"

I could feel my molars grind. "Sorry," I whispered in indication for her to continue.

She took a breath and continued. "I was so worried about what I tasted like, smelled like, that I couldn't even *feel* your touch anymore. I knew you were touching me, but my mind was so consumed with everything I had overheard that I couldn't really feel the affection or the intimacy of your touch anymore."

"That's why you started showering at night," I stated as the light bulb went off two years too fucking late. She just nodded as the realization beat inside my mind. Emily used to always shower in the morning because she needed the shock of the water to wake her up. She wasn't a morning person.

Fuck.

"That's also why you always take a quick second shower after we have sex, isn't it?"

"Yeah, it just..." She averted her eyes for this part. "I feel dirty afterwards."

I dropped my head in my hands. I couldn't look at her. My heart hurt knowing she'd overheard my stupid drunk ramblings. However, my soul was taking a beating with knowing that she had slowly pulled herself away from me these past couple of years and I hadn't even noticed.

I didn't fucking notice that she no longer leaned into my touch or greeted me at the end of the day with a kiss. I didn't notice when she started to just spread her legs for me with no hint of affection. My stupid ass ego had just thought that she wanted me so badly that she hadn't wanted any foreplay. And because I was always so eager to be inside of her, I believed it to be a win-win to leave out the foreplay and find myself immediately inside her body.

God, what a fucking asshole I was-am.

"I couldn't...can't stand for you to go down on me, Marcus." My head jerked up at that fucked-up statement. "I worry about my hygiene to the point of tears and....and I used to love to give you that pleasure, too, but my mind started ruining that for me, also. Whenever I would give you head, all I could think about was how heartbroken I felt that I still wanted you so badly after all these years that I didn't care how you came to me. I don't have a preference in how I want you. I don't care if you've showered or if you come home dirty from a job site. I don't care. I am still so attracted to you, but knowing your preferences makes me feel undesired."

"Goddamn it, Emily, I don't have a preference with you!" I shouted. *"You're my wife!* You were exempt from that stupid bullshit conversation that night!"

She just shrugged a shoulder. "I know this is all new to you, but I've spent the last two years learning how to be okay with being second and-"

I stood up, pissed all to hell, and roared, *"You're not fucking second to anyone!"* I had never felt so messed up in all my life. "Do you think I'd have married you if you weren't it for me?"

"I can't answer that. Just like you can't answer what would have happened had Stacy never adhered to her father's wishes. You might be married to her today if she hadn't ended things for the sake of money," she reasoned.

I couldn't stop myself. I grabbed the decorative lamp that sat on the goddamn decorative table stand next to the goddamn decorative armchair that I had been sitting in and threw it across the bedroom. Emily instinctively ducked as the shattered pieces rained down on the other side of the room.

She raised her head and if looks could kill... "I'll admit that I should have probably talked to you about what I had overheard long before now. I'm also aware that all of my feelings are through my perception only. However, do not stand there and act as if I'm being irrational and you're the goddamn victim in this." Emily stood up and straightened to all her five-foot-three. "How would you feel if you overheard me telling any of the girls that the only man who ever brought me drug-addicting pleasure was my ex-boyfriend before you? How would you feel if you kept listening to the conversation, and nowhere in it, I said the words 'except for Marcus'? How virile, strong, and masculine would *you* feel hearing something like that? How loved would you feel if I tacked on that the only reason that we had broken up was because *he* had needed to move on, not me?"

I couldn't breathe. The little bit I had overhead tonight with Emily just asking to *hear* more about Christopher had me irritated and feeling threatened. To actually hear her say the man before me was the best she ever had would drive me insane. Emily was a strong, beautiful, capable woman. The only thing she needed me for was to love her and pleasure her body. To even think that another man did those two things better than I ever had? I couldn't even contemplate such a thing without feeling violent.

Emily was my everything.

I would forsake every other human being on the planet if that were a condition of having her. How could she not *know* that after all these years together?

The first time I saw Emily outside the student advisory building, I had almost wrecked my truck. I had been parking and had almost forgotten to stop. She was so damn beautiful that I remember blinking uncontrollably, like I had been imagining the vision of her.

I remember it like it was this morning. She had been talking with some girl and her dark brown hair had been thrown up in a messy bun and her face had looked free of makeup from where I could see. She had been wearing a simple white t-shirt, dark jeans, and dainty, white sandals. The casual wear hadn't distracted from the hot as fuck body she'd been blessed with, though. Even from a distance, I could see she had tits meant to worship and hips made for brute force. Emily was gorgeous and her personality was a cross between sweet and wicked.

She was fucking perfect, but I was the only one who knew it, apparently.

I was still shaking with rage, but I managed to calm down long enough to put my hands on her. I grabbed her shoulders, then bent at the knees to be able to look into her face. "Emily, I can't take that night back," I started. "And I never should have been talking about other women in…that manner, no matter what, and I'm sorry. I'm so fucking sorry, Chill. I'm sorrier than you'll ever know. Still, I can't just let this be. It's not okay that you've spent the last two years thinking…" I couldn't even bring myself to say it. "It's just not okay."

The tears began again, and then she started yelling at me. "I was okay with it! Goddamn it, Marcus, I was okay with it! And I managed to be happy and satisfied with you, even if the sex did suck-" Her hands flew up and cover her mouth, her eyes rounding with the realization of what she just said. She started shaking her head and lowered her hands reaching for me. "Marcus, I didn't mean-"

I didn't stick around to hear her apology or explanation. I stormed out of our bedroom before the entire bedroom suffered the same fate as that stupid fucking lamp.

CHAPTER 4

Emily ~

I stood in front of the kitchen window, looking out into the quiet neighborhood street. It was only seven o'clock on a Saturday morning, so activity was minimal, except for the occasional jogger. I was letting my tea sit until it was strong enough to hopefully erase last night. I wasn't a coffee drinker, but I kept glancing over at Marcus' coffee maker and wondering if a hit of caffeine would give me the false sense of a good night's sleep.

To say I slept like shit last night was an understatement. Marcus had never come back to our bed, and I had been too raw, hurt, angry, and ashamed to go look for him. When I had woken up this morning, I'd gone to work on cleaning up the broken shards of what was left of the lamp. Once that had been cleaned up, I had taken another shower, brushed my teeth, and then came down for a cup of tea. The idea of having a cup of tea outside on the patio sounded soothing, so that's what I was aiming for.

Once I was satisfied with the tea, I walked outside in my worn, ratty sleep shirt, non-matching pajama pants, and bare feet. It was still a little chilly in the morning, but I didn't mind. Cold or cool weather always helped to wake me up.

Last night was like a non-stop disco light, flashing at me over and over again with everything that'd been said. I could make up all kinds of excuses for my part of the discussion, but no matter how angry or hurt I had been, I never should have said our sex life sucked because that wasn't even remotely true. I mean, sure, it lacked a lot of extras, but the sex was still great. Plus, I loved getting lost in the sensations of Marcus being inside of me.

I took a sip of tea and closed my eyes as I rested my entire body along one of the chaise lounges that made up our patio set. I didn't want to panic, but I knew Marcus and I were in a delicate position right now regarding our marriage. Everyone knew a woman's kryptonite was her self-esteem and a man's kryptonite was his sexual prowess. Fantastically, Marcus and I had

22

managed to hit both those direct targets.

I've wished several times over to go back in time before the night of Scott's visit. I've fantasized about wishing I had taken a sleeping pill, so that I'd slept through the night and had never woken up thirsty. I've fantasized about being so sleepy that I just grabbed the glass of water and walked away without hearing a word they said. I've replayed that night in my head so many different ways, so many times, but short of a full-blown lobotomy, I knew I'd never forget that night or Marcus' words.

If I was being completely honest with myself, the full truth was that I've always felt insecure around Marcus, even before that night. Since the moment he came running at me in front of the student advisory building back in college, he's intimidated me. Marcus never seemed to have any self-doubt. He always came off as super-confident. He was hot as hell, successful, funny, strong, smart…he was the complete package. Women wanted him and men envied him, and why wouldn't they?

I knew I wasn't ugly, and I worked very hard to maintain a decent figure, but Marcus was like the sun to me, so how could I not feel small or lacking around him? Still, I never blamed him for my issues because they were *my* issues. Marcus had never done anything-with the exception of that one night-to make me feel unloved or unwanted. He always seemed like he desired me. However, no matter how hot and heavy we've been, I've always kept a lot of fantasies and desires locked away. What if he thought I was weird? Or what if it changed the way he wanted me? What if my desires turned him off? All these years later, whenever Marcus walked into a room, I got butterflies in my stomach and would be in awe that he belonged to me. Who would risk losing someone so magnificent to a few unfulfilled sexual wishes?

Not this girl.

I loved my husband, and I was very aware of how lucky I was to have him. Marcus was a really good guy and I meant what I had said last night. Everything else was so good in our lives that I was fine without the romance-novel sex. I was okay without the flowers or stolen kisses.

Still, just like that night, two years ago, I couldn't pretend that last night hadn't happened, either. We were going to have to deal with this, and that meant another conversation about all my insecurities. I couldn't speak for anyone else but voicing all your fears and doubts to another human being was like touching every nerve you had with an electrical current. It was scary, intimidating, and painful as all hell.

It didn't matter that Marcus was my husband and the person who knew me best in the world. It was scarring to show someone else all your weaknesses. Here I was, married to a strong, confident man, and he had just learned that he was married to an insecure, weak woman.

Fuck. My. Life.

My eyes snapped open when I heard the sliding glass door to the patio open. I felt the bottom of my stomach drop and my heart felt like it was going to explode.

I was scared.

I was scared that Marcus was coming out here to tell me our marriage was over.

Irrational, right?

However, I couldn't help it. I mean, where were we supposed to go from here? We were in a marriage where the wife felt undesirable, and the husband felt unmanned. I voted for focusing on the good since I'd been doing it for the past couple of years anyway, but I somehow felt that Marcus would not be going that route. Marcus wasn't a coward, and lucky us, it was Saturday morning, so we didn't even have the excuse of work to put this disaster on hold. We had all day today and all day tomorrow to jack this shit up some more.

I was surprised when Marcus reached down, lifted my legs, then placed them over his lap as he sat down on the end of the chair. He wrapped one arm around the top of my knees and slipped his other hand into the left pant leg of my pajamas, then absently started rubbing my bare leg.

I wanted to cry.

I felt the tingle on the end of my nose and my eyes begin to get misty. Even when we were a mess, he was still kind. I didn't think I could speak without flat out bawling, so I remained quiet, waiting for him to begin.

He was looking at the shape of his hand underneath the fabric of my pajamas as it traveled up and down when he finally spoke. "I love you, Emily. I love you so much that I can't breathe with it sometimes." The tears escaped because there was no way I could hold them back after that. "You're the only thing in this entire world that scares me." He finally looked over at me. "I can survive anything life throws at me. Anything, with the exception of losing you." He let out a low laugh. "If you ever tried to walk out on me, I wonder at the lengths I'd go to in order to prevent that. The options are limitless and that should scare you because it scares me."

Was I unstable to say that, instead of feeling scared that he might actually contemplate murdering me, I was getting turned on as hell? Had I sunk so far down that hearing my husband suggest that he'd that kill me than lose me would actually turn me on?

I seriously need some couch time with a professional.

Seriously.

"Marcus, I know you love me-"

"Emily, I don't just love you," he said, interrupting me. "I'm in love with you like I need you to breathe. I'm in love with you like food and water are secondary to your existence in my life." He shook his head a little as if he was trying to understand how I couldn't know all this. His voice took on a hard, granite vibration. "There is no way, in this life or the next, that I'm going to lose you over this. *Over anything.*"

"Oh, Marcus, you're not going to lose me. I told you I was okay with all this. I'm happy with our life the way it is." I tried to make him see that I didn't want to lose him over this either.

The tick in his jaw looked painful. "You are out of your mind if you think I'm okay with my wife going the rest of her life sexually unfulfilled."

Men and their dicks, I swear.

"Marcus, I didn't mean what I said last night about the sex sucking." I didn't miss his small flinch at my words. "The sex part is great. When you're inside me, it's the best high in the world every single time. I swear."

"I don't want you to make do with just my dick, Chill." He threw my legs off his lap and stood up. I sat up as he paced back and forth, his hands running through his hair and down his face. "You keep saying that as if who we are and what we do is just fuck." He stopped and looked down at me. "You're my wife. I'm your husband. We are *not* fuck buddies. We are in a marriage that I intend to remain in for the rest of my fucking life. So, it's not okay if all you do is spread your legs and all I do is stick my dick in you until we're done. That's what prostitutes are fucking for."

I stood up because I didn't want to have this conversation sitting down with him towering over me. I felt weak enough as it was. "God, you act like I wanted things to turn out this way."

"Well, didn't you?" he accused. "All I've heard is how you started feeling like a consolation prize, but kudos to you, you've managed to accept it and you're fine moving on in life believing that your husband is a fucking asshole."

Now I was getting pissed. I narrowed my eyes at him. "I've never called you an asshole. You don't fucking get it, you self-centered jackass."

"Oh, because being called a jackass is so much better than being called an asshole." He threw his arms up. "That's great, Chill. That's just so fucking perfect." He went back to running his hands through his hair in frustration.

To. Hell. With. This. Shit.

"Well, now that you've told me what you've *heard*, how about you stop and actually *listen* to what I've said and am saying again? This isn't about how *I* view *you*. You have always been a good man and husband to me. I never-*ever*-said you weren't. You are gorgeous, successful, kind, generous and, yes, you have a big dick. I look at you and I am so amazed how someone who looks like you, and is as good as you are, could possibly love me. I've thought that since the first day you came up to me." The stupid tears started flowing and that just pissed me off more. "I still get butterflies in my stomach when you walk into a room, Marcus. I revel in the *existence* of you. I love you. I love you so much that I don't care if I'm first, second, or tenth in what you want in a woman. I'm just happy you want me in *any* fashion. *That's* why I'm okay without the kissing, touching, and foreplay. *I will take you any way that I can get you.* I love you so much more than I love myself or else my self-esteem wouldn't take a backseat to being with you."

"Chill-"

"No," I interrupted. "You want to make this about you and concentrate on how you aren't fulfilling all my sexual wants, but that's not what this is. This is me. *Me.* I've always had self-doubt and worried that I wasn't good enough for you. Then, one night, I overhear you telling a friend how there was ever only one woman who you were crazed for, *and it wasn't me.* I got lumped in with all the other women who you prefer fresh out of the shower."

"Goddamn it, Emily-"

"Will you just stop and fucking listen?" I rarely cursed at Marcus, but I felt like I was being scraped raw. "I am not martyring myself. I'm not trying to guilt trip you. I am telling you the truth when I tell you I am happy with our life just the way it is, regardless of how you felt about Stacy, because I love you so much that I will take *ANY* fucking scraps you want to give me." I swiped at my tears, but they just kept on coming. "And if that makes me sad and pathetic, then so be it."

I turned and ran-yes, ran-to the sliding glass door and threw it open. I ran into the house without bothering to shut the door and headed straight to our bedroom. And just like a ten-year-old, I locked myself in the bathroom. I slid down the back of the door and cried like Satan was coming for my soul.

My sobs were loud, messy, and painful. I couldn't quiet them down, even if I wanted to. However, I didn't want to. I didn't care if Marcus could hear me. I mean, it wasn't like I could lower myself or embarrass myself any farther after everything I just bared to him.

I couldn't understand.

I couldn't understand why he couldn't see that his touch made me cringe because I felt like I wasn't good enough for him, not because he wasn't good enough for me.

I felt so humiliated, and I couldn't help but feel a little resentful that I had to bare all my faults just because he wouldn't accept that what I wasn't lying when I said I was happy with how things were.

I knew I couldn't stay locked in the bathroom forever, but I irrationally wished I could. I was seriously considering laying down a bunch of towels on the floor and just crying myself to sleep when I heard Marcus knock on the door. "Emily?"

I stood up and pressed my ear to the door. "Yeah?" I was such a hiccupping mess, it's a wonder I managed to get that one word out.

"What would you do if I did cheat on you?" he asked quietly. Just when I thought this shitstorm couldn't get any more painful, he had to go and ask me that question. "Would you leave me?"

Has he? Was that why he was asking?

What the hell?

I started crying harder and I knew he could hear me through the door. "N…no…I don't know. I'm afraid my love for you might be stronger than whatever you could do to me," I shamefully admitted. "I just don't know."

Here's the thing; it was easy to say you'd leave your spouse if they ever cheated on you or abused you. However, if it actually happened, that resolve wasn't so cemented after all. At the end of the day, leaving would break up your family, no matter whose fault it was or the reason.

"Goddamn it!" he roared through the door.

And then all hell broke loose.

I stayed locked in the bathroom as I heard the sounds of furniture being destroyed amidst a slew of cursing and yelling.

I slid back down against the door as Marcus obliterated our bedroom furnishings. I knew I should go out there and save the innocent furniture, but I felt so weak and raw that I truly didn't have the energy to duck flying debris.

Hopefully, no one calls the police.

CHAPTER 5

Marcus ~

I sat on the bed, blind to all the destruction around me.

Just when I thought I couldn't get any more pissed, Emily had to go and tell me that she'd stay with me, even if I did fuck around on her.

What in the actual fuck?

My heart had actually bled for her when she had stood out on the patio and had confessed all her worries and insecurities. I knew I wasn't responsible for Emily's self-esteem issues, but if she felt like I was too good for her fifteen years into our marriage, then I sucked as a husband.

I may have spent the last fifteen years living true to our wedding vows, making sure she was provided for, taking care of her physically, and being faithful to her, but it was pretty evident that I've failed miserably with her emotionally.

I figured that as long as she smiled and didn't complain, then everything was fine.

Fuck, if I wasn't wrong.

I could admit that I wasn't one to wax on poetically all the time; that just wasn't me. I showed Emily how much I loved her by doing things for her, by being the man of the house and owning the man role. I worked hard, took care of the yard, handled anything laborious, maintained of the cars, checked on all the odd noises outside at night...I did all that shit.

Emily, in turn, worked because she wanted to and not because she had to. She cooked, cleaned, and did the laundry. But, even then, if I ever found myself coming home from a job site, I always took care of my work clothes, so she didn't have to bother. She had taken on the role of wife with ease and no complaints.

I thought everything was fucking perfect.

Last night I had been pissed that this was about our sex life, but now I wished it was *only* about our sex life. However, this was so much bigger than that. I had felt fairly confident last night that I could fix whatever was wrong in the bedroom. I was sure I could show her how attracted I was to her. I was sure I could make her forget that stupid fucking night.

That wasn't the case now. I needed to find a way to make her believe me when I told her it was the other way around. She saw me as strong, successful, and handsome, but I was *nothing* if Emily wasn't with me.

I looked around the bedroom, taking in the mess I made, and figured I should probably call my brother and apologize for all the times I judged his volatile reactions. I mean, I was the rational situation assessing one, right? I guess I should start amending that to tack on 'except when it comes to my wife' to the end.

However, right now, all that matter was that I was not going to spend the rest of the day destroying our home while Emily cried in the bathroom. "Emily, come out here," I commanded. I could hear her muffled voice, but I couldn't make out her words, and quite frankly, I didn't care what she was saying. All I wanted was her to come out of the goddamn bathroom. "Now, Emily, or so help me God, I'll break down the fucking bathroom door." And I would.

I looked up as I heard the click from the lock disengage. I watched as Emily walked out and took inventory of the mess all around us. Her eyes grew to the size of saucers as she really took note of the destruction I caused. "Marcus…" she breathed.

"Come here," I commanded again. I didn't want to talk about the furniture. I didn't want to talk about my rage or her insecurities. I didn't want to talk at all.

I wanted to fuck my wife with a need so great that I was out of my mind with it.

She slowly shuffled her bare feet until she was standing directly in front of me. I spread my legs and she automatically stepped in between them. Because I was so much taller than Em, my face was at eye-level with her chest.

Emily was wearing her customary worn t-shirt and pajama pants that she always wore to sleep. My mind drifted to how, once upon a time, we use to both sleep naked because we fucked every single night before we went to sleep. The memory had me grinding my molars to the point of pain.

I looked up at her face and it was a puffy, red, tear-filled mess.

But, fuck, she was still so beautiful.

Her shiny green orbs were reflecting embarrassment and sadness, and both made me want to punch the wall. I understood that she was sad, and I understood *why* she was sad, but she should never feel embarrassed around me. She should feel safe telling me anything-*everything*.

I reached for the hem of her shirt and pulled her closer to me. "Marcus?" The hesitancy in her voice felt like a weight on my soul.

Emily loved me, but she didn't trust me.

My wife didn't trust me and that fucking sucked.

Sure, she might trust that I didn't fuck around on her, but she didn't trust me with her feelings, thoughts, or wants, and that stung like a motherfucker.

I put my hands on either side of her waist, then grabbing the elastic waistbands of her pajama pants and panties, I slowly started to lower them down her body.

"Marcus," she whispered, "what are you doing?"

I didn't answer her. I just continued to push her clothes down her legs. I watched her pants and panties pool at her feet, and I waited with bated breath to see what she'd do now that she stood in front of me half naked.

I wanted to drop to my knees in prayer and gratefulness when she quietly lifted her feet one at a time and stepped out of her clothes.

I slowly raised my gaze from her feet to her legs to her thighs and, unfortunately, her shirt was long enough to cover that neatly trimmed triangle of hers. I continued to peruse her body, and when I got to her full, heavy tits, I saw that she was heaving with lust.

God, at least I hoped to hell it was lust and not nervousness or fear.

I didn't stop to appreciate the fullness of her chest like I wanted to. Instead, I continued until I was looking into her perfect fucking face. She still looked like a beautiful mess, but her eyes were no longer clouded with embarrassment or sadness. Emily looked flushed, but for all the right reasons.

"Marcus..." she tried again, but again, I ignored her.

I reached up, then grabbing the collar of her shirt, ripped it right down the middle until it fell off her shoulders into a rag near her pants.

Emily let out a gasp so heated and so sexy that I leaned into her and bit into the fleshy mound of her right tit until I tasted copper. *"Marcus...oh, God..."*

I grabbed her by her hips and went to feasting on her tight, harden nubs. No matter how much attention I gave each tit, it wasn't enough. I wanted both her big tits and hard nipples in my mouth at the same time.

I wanted to devour her.

She couldn't stand on her own anymore, and when I felt her hands land on my shoulders for support, I let out a growl.

I tore my mouth away from her tits and looked up at her to see her eyes closed and her head thrown back. She looked drugged and I needed that reassurance.

I quickly lifted my ass and slid my night pants down, kicking them off my ankles, and before Emily could protest, I lifted her and straddled her over my hard cock.

She wrapped her arms around my neck and automatically started rubbing herself back and forth over my hardness. I circled her body with one arm, and I used the other to tangle a wad of her hair in my hand and yank her head back, giving me full access to her neck.

I was going to mark the fuck out of her, and I didn't care how pissed off she might be later. I was on a mission. I wanted her to never doubt my need for her ever again. I wanted her to never doubt her status in my life ever again.

"You want me, Chill?"

She started rubbing herself against my cock faster. "Yes…Marcus, please…"

I let go of her hair, and lifting her, grabbed my cock, angling to the opening of her sweet, tight pussy. As soon as I felt the tip slip in, I slammed her down on my cock until there was nothing left to give her. *"Marcus…"*

Thank God she was dripping wet because she would have been torn by the force of my entry, but a sick part of me wished she had been. I didn't know how else to make her believe how much I wanted her other than to lose all sense of control and leave her battered, bruised, and thoroughly fucked to where she'd never question my need for her ever again.

Emily started moving her hips and I couldn't contain the moan that slipped through my lips. "That's it, baby. Ride my fucking cock."

She dropped her head onto my shoulder as she started riding me. "You're so deep, Marcus. You're so deep."

"You can take it, baby," I encouraged her.

Emily tightened her hold on me and started bouncing harder and faster on my cock. She mentioned last night that having me inside her was the best high she's ever felt, but I didn't think it could compare to how euphoric it felt to have her pussy wrap my cock up so tightly.

Whether it was all night long, a frantic quickie, or a tired boning, fucking Emily always felt like I belonged nowhere else. Pussy was every man's weakness, but when you were inside the woman you loved, and when you were taking what no other man will ever have, it was better than any other kind of fuck around.

"I need you cumming on my cock, baby," I groaned.

And then she hit me with some shit she's never done before. She bounced harder before making a demand of her own. "Make me."

I almost nutted right then and there.

Emily was never much of a dirty talker. I was usually the one throwing random shit out there, but I made sure never to get too filthy with her. She was my wife. Even when I was screwing her hard and deep, I still did my best to respect her.

I was too stunned to respond, and before I knew it, she was taking her climax. She was riding my cock like she was a professional lap dancer and world peace hinged on her getting off.

Fuck, it was hot.

She was hot. Still, there was no way I was going to let her make herself cum. That was my fucking job.

Plus, I was still feeling…uh, edgy about her comments on our sex life. *I* was going to make her cum, not the other way around. "No way you're doing this without me, baby." I grabbed onto her hips and using all the strength I had in my hands, wrists, and arms, I started lifting her and slamming her back down onto my cock.

Emily threw her head back and screamed, *"Marcus!"*

Fuck. I couldn't remember the last time she really screamed out my name during sex. Sure, she's called it out lots, and lots of times. She'd moan my name when she was cumming, but screaming? It's been ages since she's *screamed* for me.

Like everything else I've apparently taken for granted, I always assumed the size of my dick was enough to get her off. I wasn't being a braggart, but my nine inches of thick dick almost always got the job done. However, I was starting to see the difference between just making Emily cum and making Emily cum *for me*. "That's it, baby. Take my cock until you cream all over me."

I was so hell bent on making sure she couldn't walk afterwards, I kept lifting her and slamming her back down on my dick as hard as I could. I was so turned on that I didn't know how much longer I was going to last. I needed to push Emily over the edge.

I leaned in and took a chuck of her heavy tit into my mouth and bit down. *Hard.*

"Oh, God…oh, God…Marcus…"

I started sucking on the flesh in my mouth and drove my cock up in her hot pussy as hard as I could. Within seconds, I could feel the clamping around me, and I knew she was on the verge of exploding all over me. My teeth held her tit prisoner as she started wailing and crying out her orgasm.

"Oh, God…yes…oh, Marcus…please don't stop…"

"Never, Chill. I'll never stop fucking your sweet, tight cunt," I assured her.

Within seconds, her pussy took hold of my dick in a hold so tight that I clamped my teeth on her tit harder. I felt the hot gush of cream soak my cock from her orgasm. *"Yes…Marcus…"*

I had to free her tit as I threw my head back and growled out my own release. I drove up into her body so hard, had I not had a hold of her hips, I would have bucked her off.

Emily dropped her head on my shoulder and kept her arms wrapped around my neck as she came down from her orgasm. I continued to hold on to her hips and worked on controlling my hormones and thoughts.

After a couple of minutes, Emily pulled back and started running her fingers through my hair as she looked at me. "That felt good. Thank you."

I snorted. "No need to thank me, Chill. Having your pussy wrapped around my cock is always *my* pleasure, baby."

Suddenly, she looked sad, and her eyes reflected nothing but regret when she spoke. "I know we have a lot to talk about still, but…but can we just…put it on hold for right now." She gave me a small smile. "We have a bit of a mess to clean up."

I wanted to demand we talk, but I wanted her happier more. "Sure thing, Em."

CHAPTER 6

Emily ~

It took most of Saturday to clean up the disaster Marcus had made in the bedroom yesterday. I could admit, I let the sex distract me from the shock of seeing Marcus lose his shit like that. Marcus was the calm, cool brother. Marcus assessed situations and was able to calculate the best course of action even in the midst of chaos. It was one of the things that I loved about him. His confidence and calmness made me feel safe. If we were being chased by murderers, I would follow him anywhere, no questions asked.

So, hearing him destroy everything around him last night from the safety of the bathroom had me completely dumbfounded. Everyone knew Matthew was the hotheaded one out of the Maxwell brothers.

Who knew?

When he had called me out into the bedroom, I honestly hadn't known what to expect. When I had walked out and saw him calmly sitting on the bed, I had been slightly baffled. That was until I had noticed his chest was heaving and he hadn't been so calm after all.

When he had said the words that commanded that I go to him, I had instantly felt wetness pooling between my legs. I was no different from any number of other women who got turned on by the alpha in her male.

Marcus had still had some aggression flowing through his veins when he had called me over and I had been eager to help him get it all out. I had wanted him to fuck me like he was out of his mind with need.

Christ, I had never cum so hard.

It wasn't that I needed Marcus to be out of control all the time. I didn't even know if I approved of the violence to our furniture, but he had been displaying so much passion-albeit it was violent and had nothing to do with love-but it had not been boring.

It hadn't been the same Saturday night at the Maxwell residence. I had *believed* his grunts and moans. I had *believed* his dirty promises.

God, what had I been thinking? Any woman would be lucky to have Marcus. I was letting my insecurities make it appear as if Marcus was lacking in some way and he wasn't. He really wasn't. He was damn near perfect.

Sure, he had his quirks and minor habits that would annoy me, but compared to everything else he did and the man he was, who cared?

I let out a deep breath and went back to answering some emails. I normally didn't work on Sundays, but Marcus and I had converted the sitting room into a shared office space, and it was hard not to check emails and do the little things while at home. It was work, but it didn't feel like work when it was all optional.

"Working?"

I looked up and saw Marcus standing in the doorway. "Just thought I'd go through my emails. You know, just seeing what's there to greet me tomorrow morning," I answered.

He nodded his head in complete understanding. He was guilty of addressing work issues during the weekends, too. He lazily strolled into the room. "I was going to ask you if you wanted some lunch." He kept walking until he was behind my chair. I felt his hands on my shoulders before I felt the whisper of his breath at my ear. "But I'm thinking I'd rather have *you* for lunch."

My breath hitched and the raspy heat of his voice had me thinking that was a great idea. "Oh, yeah?"

He swiveled my chair to face him. Instead of answering me, he started unbuttoning his jeans. I could feel my blood heat as I stared at his fingers working his pants undone. The beginning and end of it all was that I just wished I turned Marcus on half as much as he turned me on. One look, one kiss, one comment, and I was ready.

His jeans were unbuttoned, and he was pulling out his dick in all its massive glory. It was already semi-hard and quickly growing to its full length and width. Marcus had an impressive cock; it was just so long and thick. It was then that I realized how much I missed sucking him off.

All this talk about everything that was lacking in our sex life, sucking his dick was one that we both suffered for. I used to love taking him into my mouth and hearing him praise my skills and come undone down my throat. I knew a lot of women felt like fellatio was a debasing act, but not me. I wanted to bring my husband pleasure. I wanted to be the woman he used to make all his sexual fantasies come true. I wanted to be the woman who made all his sexual encounters mind-blowing. If that meant he needed to get rough, if that meant he needed to get dirty, if that meant he needed to talk to me like I was a whore, so be it.

In this moment, I wanted nothing more than to take his cock into my mouth and suck on him until he lost his load down my throat, on my face, in my hair…wherever.

I didn't care.

I. Did. Not. Care.

I looked up at him as I took over and started circling his cock with my hand. I watched as Marcus briefly closed his eyes. I knew he was hoping for a blowjob. I couldn't remember the last time I sucked his dick, but I was sure he remembered.

I sat up as erect as I could and finally wrapped my lips around the head of his dick. The second I closed my mouth around him, Marcus let out a moan so sexy that I felt like I was the best cock sucker who ever lived.

It was all the encouragement I needed to start taking his length up and down my throat. I closed my eyes and erased every thought in my head. I sucked, licked, and nipped his cock in all the ways I could think of. My tongue played on the ridge underneath and my lips cushioned the head of his dick. "Fuck, Em," he panted. "That feels so fucking good, baby." I felt his hands tangle in my hair, and I wanted to scream at him to grip my hair tighter. I wanted to beg him to fuck my mouth. I wanted to demand so many things, but my confidence wasn't there yet.

It wasn't very long before I could feel his cock expand in my mouth. I knew he was going to cum soon, so I upped my efforts. "Keep sucking my cock, baby. I'm going to cum."

Hell yeah.

A few minutes later, I felt the squirt of his release shock my taste buds, and I swallowed and gulped everything he had to give. *"Fuck...Emily...baby..."*

I continued to lick his cock clean until he started going soft in my hand. It had been so long since I've given Marcus a blowjob that I was actually feeling kind of shy. For some reason, I felt unsure and couldn't quite look at him. I wanted so badly to continue riding the high, but my mind started wandering like all women who were screwed up in the head, and I sadly began to wonder how my blowjobs compared to Stacy's.

I know...stupid, right?

Marcus must have sensed the change because his voice was very careful as he tucked himself back into his pants. "Chill...are...are you alright?"

No!

God, I wanted to scream at him that I wasn't fucking alright. I'd just blown my husband and I was worried that I couldn't compare to a woman that he used to fuck over *fifteen* years ago.

I wiped at the edges of my mouth as I turned my chair back around to face the desk. "Yeah, I just gotta get back to these emails, is all."

I felt Marcus step back. It was suddenly cool where, thirty seconds ago, it had been all heat. "You have got to be kidding me," he mumbled right before he clearly stated, "This is bullshit, Emily."

I took a deep breath and stood up to face him. *Here we go again.* "My feelings aren't bullshit, Marcus. At the end of the day, you can say whatever you want about what you meant and what you mean, and a whole host of other things that you think will fix this-will fix *me*. However, here's the bottom line; two years ago, I laid in bed all night replaying your words over, and over in my mind and I made a logical-instead of emotional-decision to stay in my marriage after what I heard. For two years, we didn't hug, kiss, caress, touch, explore-*nothing*-and you didn't even notice. Either that or you were perfectly okay with all that being absent from our relationship." My body was shaking with resentment. "Now, all of a sudden, you find out why I changed, and you want to feel offended by it. Well, tell me the reason why *you* changed? Tell me what the catalyst was that made it okay for you not to crave *my* touch? What made it okay for you to not feel the need to touch *me*? What made it okay for two fucking years to go by before you said anything?"

Marcus looked stunned and it pissed me off more.

He kept insisting on dragging my deepest insecurities and issues to light, but then belittles them because I should *just know* that he loves me. Yet, when it's his turn to come clean, he balks.

"You're such a jerk, Marcus. I'm not the one who wants to keep having these conversations. I'm not the one trying to put all this shit front and center. I keep telling you that I'm fine and I'm okay with what I think and what I feel, but, of course, you know better." The goddamn tears started *a-fucking-gain*. "Now I'm something that has to be fixed because you can't just let it go." I stepped around him to hide in our bedroom like the coward I was. I stopped at the doorway and Marcus was still standing still. "Before, I just felt like I was runner-up whenever we had sex. Now...now that you've pulled all this shit out of me, I feel embarrassed. I feel embarrassed about my wants and needs. I feel embarrassed in front of *you*." I took off towards the bedroom before he could respond.

Of course, he came after me, though.

I was pacing the bedroom floor when he came through the door. It wasn't thirty seconds later that I wished I had never asked him those questions. "I thought we were good, Emily. That is, until I came home Friday and I heard you telling the girls that our sex life was *fine*." He said the word 'fine' with a sneer. "And then you go on to beg Teri to tell you more about some guy she's been fucking."

I lowered my head as I shook it in disbelief.

God, I was such a fucking idiot.

I finally looked back up and I wasn't sure what he saw in my eyes, but Marcus stopped cold. "So, this isn't even about me or us or what's been lacking in our marriage. You got butthurt because I wasn't singing your praises to the girls. Your ego got dented because I wasn't gushing about what a sex god you were." I sat down and put my head in my hands. "I'm such a goddamn fool," I mumbled to myself.

"Chill-"

I stood back up and let loose on the honesty. "I told the girls that our sex life was fine because, in my opinion, that's the truth. It *is* fine. And, yes, I asked to hear more about Christopher because I loved knowing that there's a guy out there who could make a woman feel that beautiful and desired. I wasn't interested in the size of his dick or how skilled he is with his tongue. I wanted to hear more about how he made Teri *feel* because *that's* what I cared about in her story."

There was a tick in his jaw. "It still didn't sit well with me hearing you say our sex life was *fine.*"

I scoffed. "Trust me, it is way better to hear your sex life being described as fine versus hearing your husband talk about how the best sex of his life *isn't* with you."

"And is the best sex of your life with me?"

And because the honesty was still flowing freely…"You still don't get it." I let out another deep breath. "No matter what I believe about how you view me, you…you are still the most beautiful man I have ever seen. You are gorgeous, strong, and have a body that men in their 20s would envy. The affection might suck and the foreplay nonexistent, but when you're inside me, nothing else compares. It's the best feeling in the world to me. There's nowhere else I'd rather be and there's no one else I'd rather be with. I've never laid with you with another man on my mind. I've never compared you to one of my exes because there's no comparison." I felt so stupid and pathetic as I poured my heart out, but I didn't stop. "I feel in awe of you, and I thank God every day that you found something in me worth marrying. That's why it only took one night to decide to stay with you, no matter how you feel about Stacy. I love and want you so much that being second still feels like coming in first."

"You're not fucking second!" he roared, angry and frustrated.

However, all I felt was exhausted. "Just leave me alone, Marcus. We're getting nowhere and I'm so tired of this stupid conversation. Let's just agree to disagree and move the hell on."

He stomped over to stand in front of me, and then lowered himself on his haunches, so that he was face-to-face with me. He took my chin in his hand-none too gently, might I add-and practically growled in my face. "I'll admit this is a fucked-up situation, but you are out of your fucking mind if you think I'll *ever* leave you alone. And you're seriously fucked in the head if you think I'm going to drop this issue and let you continue on thinking that you're not the best fuck I've ever had."

I couldn't help the surprised look on my face. I've never met this Marcus before. The Marcus that I knew was the calm one. "I don't see-"

Marcus shook his head to signal that I quit talking. "I created this mess with my careless words, and I'll fix it, Emily. I don't care what I have to do. I don't care what it takes."

I could feel all the fight leave my body. "What if it can't be fixed?" I whispered.

"It can be because there's no other option as far as I'm concerned." He shook my head with his grip on my chin. "There's no way in hell I'm going to-" Marcus made sure I held his gaze. "There's just no fucking way, Chill."

I just nodded because I didn't know what else to do. I didn't necessarily agree with him that this could be fixed, but I knew I didn't want to fight anymore. "I think I'm just going to lie down and read for the rest of the day. Tomorrow's going to be busy and I just…" I let my sentence trail off because we both knew I was full of shit.

Marcus must have felt sorry for me because he let go of my chin and stood up, giving me space. "Fine, I'll let you…relax for the rest of the day," he said, taking a deep breath. "But at some point, we're going to have to revisit this, Chill."

I looked down. "I know, Marcus, just not today, okay?"

I heard him sigh again, and rather than answer me, I heard him walk out of our bedroom. I fell back on the bed and secretly wished he had stayed.

CHAPTER 7

Marcus ~
Today was the day of the Maxwell employee appreciation barbecue, and for the first time since its conception, I didn't want to be here.

Every year I held a companywide barbecue, Christmas party, and appreciation dinner, and I've always had a great time at each event, but today felt forced.

For starters, I showed up alone because Emily had been struggling with getting ready. I knew she was having some sort of self-esteem appearance meltdown when nothing she picked to wear had been good enough. She had also showered twice because she claimed her hair wouldn't 'cooperating', whatever the fuck that meant.

All week had been tense and uncomfortable, and I've hated every minute of it. We tip-toed around each other when we weren't outright avoiding one another. Nighttime was the worst. Every time I went to touch her or fuck her, all I could think about was what *she* was thinking about, and it killed each one of my erections. So, like a coward, I would just roll over and go to sleep.

So, after a week of not really talking, no sex, no affection, and watching her struggle to feel pretty this morning, I was in a foul mood. I left the house so pissed off that I told her she'd better show up within the hour or I was going to go back to the house and drag her out by her uncooperative hair in whatever state of dress she was in.

She told me to go fuck myself.

Emily never spoke to me that way...or, at least, she never *used* to speak to me that way. It almost had me bending her over the bed and fucking her until she wasn't physically capable of going to the barbecue. Instead, I had counted to ten, then slammed the front door on my way out.

I was doing my best to mingle, but every time someone asked me where Emily was, I wanted to punch something.

I really owed my brother an apology for my judgments on his temper.

"Holy shit, I think I see my future wife, gentlemen," Jacob Resnik announced to our little circle. He was a nice kid who's been with the company a little over four months. He was a hard worker if a little bit open and wild.

John Phillips, Mark Murry, Eric Benter, all employees of mine, and I all turned our heads to see who Jacob was talking about. The only person I saw walking through the private park was Emily.

"Who are you talking about?" John, one of my site foremen, asked.

"Who am I talking about? Does marriage make men blind or something?" Jacob nodded his head in a direction that had me ready to blow. "I'm talking about the brunette goddess that just arrived."

I knew he was talking about Emily as she was currently the only brunette goddess walking through the park towards us. She was dressed in a white blouse that tied in the front and rested over a flowing peach skirt that reached her ankles. She wore a pair of matching white sandals and she finally opted for wearing her hair up in a loose bun.

She looked like an untouchable gypsy.

I didn't blame Jacob for being spellbound, but she was still my wife. I tried to calm my voice the best I could. "That's my wife, Jacob."

I looked back over at the kid and his eyes were bugging out of his head. *"That's* your wife?"

"Yes," I bit out.

"Goddamn, Boss. How in the world do you function?" Jacob whistled.

I glanced back at Emily really quickly, hoping to end this conversation before she made it to our group. "What do you mean?"

Jacob cocked his head and looked at me like I was a complete imbecile. "Seriously? Dude, if that were my wife, I wouldn't be able to get out of bed long enough to hold down a job, much less build a company." Jacob shook his head a little. "The world would have to drag me away from her side daily." He clapped me on the shoulder. "You're one lucky sonofabitch, Marcus."

Emily approached just as Jacob removed his hand from my shoulder. She smiled at the men. "Hello, John, Mark, Eric."

They all returned her greeting just as Jacob stuck his hand out to introduce himself. "Jacob Resnik."

Emily smiled at him, too, and I swear to God, I wanted to punch him in his face. "Emily Maxwell. It's nice to meet you. I don't have the opportunity to meet all of Marcus' employees often."

"The pleasure is all-"

I couldn't stand it any longer. "Okay, that's enough. Go introduce yourself elsewhere, Jacob."

He laughed and threw Emily a flirty wink. "Sure thing, Boss."

John, Mark, and Eric all chuckled at Emily's confused expression. "Well, that was rude," she pointed out.

"So was telling me that he had plans to make you his future wife," I countered. The guys really started laughing, and Emily and I were polite enough to let it go as a joke. Still, with everything going on, neither of us took it as the joke it was supposed to be.

Fuck this shit.

I nodded my head towards the concession building that was positioned in the middle of the park. "Want to go with me and check on the waters and beers and stuff?"

"Uh, sure," she agreed, then we started walking in silence.

I booked this particular park every year because it was beautifully manicured, and the concession building was easily stocked and accessed. The park's personnel were great and were a tremendous help in making the barbecue a success.

As we made our way through the park, I could see Rebecca Stalt making her way over to us, and it was all I could do not to groan. She had a friend with her, and while that should reassure me, it didn't. Her friend looked like a blonde Barbie wannabe, and I just didn't need this shit right now.

"Marcus. Emily," Rebecca greeted. "This is my plus-one," she said, gesturing to her friend. "My friend, Malory Milton."

I've recently suspected that Rebecca's developed a little bit of a crush on me, and while she hasn't done anything over obvious or inappropriate, I knew she found me attractive. I didn't need this shit right now. Especially, with Emily feeling all out of sorts. Still, what the fuck was I supposed to do?

"Hello, Rebecca," I said, returning the greeting. "It's nice to meet you, Malory." I wrapped my arm around Emily's waist. "This is my wife, Emily."

Emily smiled at the women. "It's good to see you again, Rebecca. Nice to meet you, Malory."

Malory tittered like a fool. "Well, I hope you guys don't mind me crashing your company party."

"Nonsense," Emily assured her. "That's what the plus-one is for."

"If you'll ladies excuse us, we need to check on the..." I waved towards the concession building. "Emily and I were just-"

"Oh," Rebecca exclaimed, her eyelashes fluttering a bit. "We didn't mean to keep you. We'll see you around later, Marcus."

I felt Emily stiffen and I wanted to fire Rebecca right then and there. Instead, I went for reassurance. "Sure, if I'm not too busy trying to get my wife somewhere private." I let the statement hang in the air as I ushered Emily along.

We finally reached the concession building when Emily spoke. "I always knew she had a thing for you." However, there was no emotion in her voice at all. She might as well have been talking about the weather and that bothered me. Emily had no reason to be jealous, but there should be some sort of emotion in her voice when she was talking about another woman having a thing for her husband, shouldn't there?

I opened the backdoor for Emily to walk through as I followed behind her. "She can have a'thing for me all she wants. I don't see anyone but you,

Chill."

"Did you need any help, Mr. Maxwell?" I turned to see Sue, one of the park's personnel, walking towards us.

"No, thank you, Sue. Mrs. Maxwell and I were just checking on a couple of items." I smiled to soften my curtness.

"Okay, well, let me know if you guys need anything." She turned to go back to attending the window.

I practically pushed Emily into the storage room. "What the hell, Marcus?"

I wanted to shout at her, *'I'm losing my fucking mind, that's what the hell!'*, but I just took her face in my hands and slammed my lips down on hers.

Thank Christ, she opened up and started kissing me back. I walked her backwards until something suspended her movement. I didn't dare stop kissing her to look up, but whatever it was, I wanted to give it thanks for helping me trap Emily in my arms.

I surrendered her lips and started kissing my way down her neck. "Marcus," she moaned. "We can't be doing this-"

I nipped at her neck and took as much of one of her tits in my hand as I could. "Bullshit."

Emily was verbally putting up a protest, but she wasn't making any effort to stop me physically, so I was counting that as a win. "Babe, we shouldn't...*oh, God...*"

I pushed up against her, so she could feel how hard my dick was. "Say yes, Chill. God, baby, please say yes," I begged.

"Say yes to *what*, exactly?"

"Let me flip that skirt up, spread your legs, and fuck your tight pussy," I clarified for her.

Emily let out a moan so desperate that I just knew she was dripping wet. Maybe I've been underestimating my wife all these years. Maybe what I had deemed as respect in the bedroom was what she saw as me holding back. "Marcus, we can't. I'll...you'll be dripping...I'll be a mess..."

I raised my head and took her chin in my hand. Her beautiful green eyes were clouded with lust, belying her words. "If I thought you'd let me, my cum would be flowing out of every fuckhole you have, Chill. And I wouldn't give a damn if everyone in this park *knew* it."

Her eyes dilated and she looked high off the idea. Then she breathed something that stopped my pulse. "Y...you want t...to fuck me in the ass, Marcus?"

Hell yeah, I wanted to fuck her in her ass.

In fifteen years, I've never asked, and she's never offered. Maybe I've been a pussy all these years, but I've always let Emily lead in the bedroom. I never wanted to ask anything of her that might make her uncomfortable. It was one of the reasons I never pushed for anything dirty with her. Being inside Emily was heaven enough, so I never bothered asking for more, but now...

"Emily, I want to fu-" The door opened, and it was like ice water on a hot fire.

Goddamn it.

"Oh, I'm so sorry, Mr. Maxw…Mrs…*oh, God,*" Sue exclaimed as we heard the door shut with a slam.

The silence was deafening for a few seconds before I closed my eyes and rested my head on Emily's chest. "Fuck."

I could feel the vibrations of Emily's laugh. "It's probably for the best, Marcus. Let's go before the poor girl dies of mortification."

I smiled as I lifted my head to meet Em's eyes. "Continue this later?"

A blush spread across her face, and it was endearing to see her feel shy when ten seconds ago she was asking me if I wanted in her ass. *God, I loved this woman.* "Yeah, we can…uh, talk about this at home."

I pulled away from her, but I wasn't done yet. "Em, I know we still have a lot to work out and…I just want you to know that I don't think a quick fuck is going to fix everything. When I go after you, it's simply just because I want you, okay?"

She took on a serious look and nodded. "I know, Marcus, but can we just get through today without…just without?"

I nodded and we made our way back to the barbecue. It wasn't a half hour later of mingling that I saw Teri arrive with some guy. My stomach churned as I took in his youthful appearance and deduced that he was probably the legendary Christopher. I nodded my head towards Teri. "Where's the rest of the crew?"

Emily's face lit up when she spotted Teri. "Jackie and Cyn couldn't make it this year. Cyn and Martin are visiting his parents and Jackie said both the girls are sick with the flu, so…"

"Hey, Emily," Teri greeted as she, and who I presumed was Christopher, finally reached us. "Hey, Marcus."

I gave her a hug and a kiss on her cheek after Emily released her. "Hey, Teri."

I hated to admit it, but Teri was all aglow when she introduced Christopher. "Emily, Marcus, I'd like to introduce you to my friend, Christopher Caruso."

Before Emily or I could voice our salutations, Christopher wrapped his arm around Teri's waist, and yanking her body to his, nuzzled her neck. "I'm not your friend, baby."

Teri smirked. "No? Then what are you?"

The fucker kissed her forehead before answering, "I'm whatever you want me to be, but it better be a shit ton more than just a friend, Tee."

Emily cleared her throat. "It's a pleasure to meet you, Christopher. Teri's told me a lot about you."

Christopher took her outstretched hand. "It's a pleasure to meet you, too, Emily. Teri has told me a lot about you, Jackie, and Cynthia. It feels like I

already know you."
  Fuck this dude.

CHAPTER 8

Emily ~

Christopher was gorgeous, and Teri hadn't been exaggerating about his attentiveness towards her. You could actually *feel* his affections for her.

I was snapped out of my momentary trance when Marcus stretched his hand out towards Christopher. "Nice to meet you, Christopher. I'm Marcus, Emily's husband."

Christopher took Marcus' hand and shook. "Good to meet you. I hope you don't mind me crashing your barbecue. However, it was either crash your party or spend the day without Teri." He gave Marcus a universal male smirk. "And that wasn't going to happen."

As ever, Marcus was his polite self. "Nah, man, it's fine. Any guest of Teri's is always welcomed with us."

"Thanks," Christopher replied.

"Marcus!" We all turned to see one of Marcus' retired employees flag him down.

"Daniel," Marcus acknowledged back. "Please excuse me. I gotta go play host." Marcus leaned down and kissed my cheek before walking towards Daniel and his wife to catch up.

I turned my attention back to Teri and Christopher. "Come on, let's go find a table, so we can sit down and drink."

Teri chuckled. "Don't you mean sit down and eat?"

"That's exactly what I meant," I laughed.

The three of us made our way to an empty park table. The party planning company that Marcus used had set up a bunch of classic round tables that they had scattered throughout our reserved area of the park but sitting at one of the actual park benches felt more casual.

Teri and I took our seats, but Christopher remained standing. "What did you ladies want to drink? Eat?"

I smiled up at him. I mean, how could I not? So far, he was everything

Teri had claimed him to be. "I already ate, but I'll take a Corona, please." I had eaten a sandwich at home before I had arrived at the park.

"I'll take the same, please," Teri requested. "Lemons with both."

I watched as he kissed the top of her head before heading off to the concession building. I shook my head in suspicion. "Teri, you guys don't look like you're just having sex. You guys look like you're in love."

She let out a laugh. "Trust me, Em, we are *not* in love. He's just…that's him. Whether serious or casual, the woman he's with is the *only* woman he's with when he's with her, ya know."

"Must be a gift because he acts completely besotted with you," I protested.

She sighed. "I admit, it feels unreal, but…Em, he's just…*a lot.*"

"He seems great," I agreed.

"So, really quick, before Chris gets back, what's up with you and Marcus?"

My face had to be showing my surprise. How could she know something was wrong? "What do you mean?"

Teri threw her head back and let out a full laugh. When she was finally able to compose herself, she had me stunned. "Because he actually *growled* when Chris shook your hand, Em."

Stunned, I tell you.

"No, he did not," I argued.

"Yes, he did, Em. It's been fifteen years, and I've never seen Marcus act jealous. So, what's going on?"

Now wasn't the time to get into mine and Marcus' issues. Even if I did have time, this thing between us felt too deep and personal to share with the girls. It wasn't that I didn't trust them, but this wasn't just a personal problem I was having. This mess included Marcus just as much as it did me and I didn't feel comfortable telling anyone Marcus' business. It felt intrusive and tinged on the edges of betrayal.

"We had a fight earlier and he's a man…" I shrugged my shoulders as I simplified the problem.

Teri rolled her eyes. "Amen."

Christopher made it back with our drinks and it was hard not to feel like a third wheel as he handed me my beer. Even though I wasn't really hungry, I grabbed a chip off the plate of random snacks Christopher had brought back with him. I watched enviously as he sat next to Teri but positioned himself, so that he had one leg on either side of the bench and was able to nestle Teri in between his legs.

"So, do you have to go play hostess to Marcus' host?" Teri asked. Previously, with Jackie and Cynthia in attendance at these things, they all kept each other company if I had to meet someone or stand with Marcus.

"Nah, he can handle it," I threw back all cavalier-like.

Teri raised her brows at me. "Okay."

I turned my attention to Christopher. "It's really great to finally meet you.

While Teri's told us a lot about you, I don't think she's ever mentioned what you do for a living." I let out a small laugh as I realized how intrusive I sounded. "And feel free to tell me anything or everything is none of my business."

Christopher let out a genuine laugh. "It's okay. Teri's told me all about you girls and I'm very aware of how open and close you ladies all are, Emily." He placed a sweet kiss on the side of Teri's face before answering my question. "I'm a corporate attorney. That's how I met Teri. Her firm hired me to go over some stuff."

I was praying that my mouth wasn't hanging open to the ground. I was so sure he was going to say a male stripper or model or sex god. Hmm, an attorney…who knew? I put on what I hoped was a smile. "Well, it really is great to finally meet you." I winked at Teri as I spoke to Christopher. "I don't think my friend here has gone a day without that stupid, cheesy grin on her face."

Teri threw a celery stick at me.

Christopher pulled Teri closer to him if that was even possible. "And I hope to keep it there," he said wickedly.

I knew Teri was insisting that it was just sex, but the way he looked at her said otherwise. Maybe he should become a Hollywood actor instead of work as an attorney if that's the case. To hell with it. I was going to ask, but only because I knew Teri didn't give a shit. "So, Christopher, Teri tells me that you have this voodoo, magical way of making her feel like she's the most beautiful female on the planet. Explain your secret ways to me."

This time, he really started laughing. His laugh was so genuine that it was infectious and had me and Teri grinning from cheek-to-cheek. He looked at me with a sparkle in his friendly brown eyes. "It's not a secret and there's no voodoo or magic involved."

I pointed my index finger at him. "Uh, that's where I beg to differ, good sir. Teri's a hardnosed, no nonsense, ball-busting female, and since she started getting naked with you, it's like she's walking around in a hail of glitter, unicorns, and orgasmic bliss." I leaned in further towards the couple. "Shit like that involves voodoo or magic or...wait, did you sell your soul to Satan for those talents?"

The man started laughing harder as Teri was telling me to shut the hell up. "I promise you, I am not involved with the occult, nor do I practice magic, or participate in any voodoo rituals."

"Then what's got my girl all sprung over here," I asked.

"For the love of God, Emily!" Teri screeched.

I ignored her and awaited Christopher's answer. "I'm waiting here."

He was able to answer after he calmed down. "Teri's doesn't scare easily. The sexiest, most alluring thing about her is how she gives herself over to me openly and freely. She trusts me with her body, and that power over her blinds me to everything around me but her."

I felt like I couldn't breathe as I watched Teri lean back into him. It was all I could do to contain the flood of emotions threatening to erupt inside me. Teri and Christopher had no commitment to one another, yet they shared a trust that I knew didn't exist between me and Marcus.

I didn't trust Marcus with my body. There was no disguising that fact. My insecurities and his fond memories of Stacy were a huge brick wall between what I desired and what I actually had. When Marcus had gotten filthy in the storage room of the concession stand earlier and had talked about wanting to cum in all my fuckholes, I had almost let him. His words had me so turned on that I was willing to let him do just that very thing to me. He normally didn't say things like that, and I knew he was just as equally shocked when I had asked him if he wanted to fuck me in the ass. Our sex life, up to this point, had always been polite. Even when we'd been frantic for each other when we'd been younger, we always focused on trying to make love and be in love instead of raw, uninhibited fucking.

Maybe the reason Stacy remained in his memories was because she had trusted him with her body and let him feed on all his sexual desires and fantasies.

Christopher snapped me out of my musing when he stood up. "More drinks, Ladies?"

Teri side-eyed him. "Like you have to ask?"

"How AA would it look if we asked you to just bring back an ice chest full of beers?" It made no sense for him to have to get up every few minutes to serve us.

Christopher chuckled. "Very AA, seeing as we have children in attendance."

"Yeah, those little buggers sure know how to keep shit in sober mode," I sighed.

Teri laughed. "Girls' night is at my place next. You can get shitfaced then."

Christopher just shook his head. "I'll be back in a few."

As soon as I felt he was out of earshot, I whisper-yelled at Teri, "Holy Mary, Mother of God, Teri. What the hell?"

She laughed. "What?"

"I know he's a few years younger than us, but how are you not in love with that man?" I mean, seriously.

Teri shrugged a shoulder. "Because I'm just not. What we have is too good to mess up with love or feelings."

"But...but I don't understand," I stammered. "He looks like he feels a whole lot."

"He's not in love with me, Em. That's just him," she insisted again. "He's very intense. It has nothing to do with having feelings for me. When we first met, he was doing his lawyer thing, and he was so enthralling and magnificent that I knew he would be a great fuck. That's why I didn't hesitate when he asked me out." Christopher made his way back before I could question Teri any further. However, I sure as hell was going to get with her later next week to continue my badgering of stuff that was clearly none of my business.

He handed us our beers before he sat down in the same exact position as he was before. It was like he couldn't stand to not be touching Teri. What a horrible friend I was to be so jealous of his yearning for her. *Ugh.*

Christopher looked over at me. "So, I know your husband has to play host to all these people, but maybe we could all go out to dinner together or have a barbecue at Teri's, or something. I'd really like to meet Cynthia, Jackie, and their husbands, too."

Teri was either stupid, blind, crazy, or all three to think that Christopher was just fucking her. While he may not love her, the man definitely liked her. I smiled. "I think that would be great."

He nuzzled his face in her hair. "What about you, babe? Is that cool with you?"

If Teri said yes, she was going to get an olive to the forehead. Meeting all of us-husbands include-would mean way more than just fucking. "I'm down. Since none of my friends are fools, it should be a good time. But-*ow! What the hell?"*

I narrowed my eyes at her. "We *will* be having lunch next week, *Teresa."*

Christopher rubbed the spot on her forehead where the olive connected. "I take it lunch is code for Emily wanting to grill you over our relationship, but she can't right now because I'm here?"

Teri narrowed her eyes back at me. "No. It just means we're overdue for a lunch date."

He snorted. "Yeah, and I'm not addicted to…" Christopher trailed off as he whispered the rest of his sentence in Teri's ear, and by the way Teri's face flushed, I'd say he was claiming to be addicted to some serious shit.

I knew I was going to have to slap some sense into her soon. So far, all I've heard were her assumptions of Christopher's personality. She's never once said that she's flat out asked him how he saw their relationship and I was pretty sure she really needed to.

Christopher looked back at me a little sheepishly. "On a scale of one to ten, how rude would it be if I whisked her away from you after only being here about an hour?"

I grinned. "It's been too long already, I take it?"

"I need to constantly remind her why she keeps me around," he grinned back.

"Chris!" Teri shook her head. "Don't mind him, Em. He can go a few hours without-"

"No, Teri, I can't. I really, really can't," he insisted as he gathered her closer.

I couldn't help but laugh at them. "It's okay. Really, Teri. If I had a choice between being at a barbecue with tons of people I didn't know and hot, sweaty, porn sex…well, I'd choose the hot, sweaty, porn sex, too."

Christopher lifted a dominant brown brow. "What do you know about hot, sweaty, porn sex?"

"I have cable," I scoffed in mock indigence.

He genuinely smiled at me. "Of course, you do, sweet girl."

I waved my hand at them in a shooing motion. "Go on and get out of here, you two crazy kids. Go enjoy the benefits of a home without children or parents."

Teri smirked at me. "Thanks, Mom."

I stayed seated as they both stood up. Christopher went to gather the plate and empty beer bottles. "Oh, I can get-"

He cut me off. "Not going to happen." He winked at me before walking off. "It was nice meeting you, Emily. Marcus, too."

I smiled as I watched them both walked towards the park trashcans, and then make their way to his car, all the while trying not to feel jealous.

CHAPTER 9

Marcus ~

I looked over at Emily as she headed in my direction, and when I looked around further, I didn't see Teri or Christopher. I knew I had been less than cordial when Teri had introduced him, but considering everything that was going on, it was hard to warm up to a man who had my wife interested in his perfectly emotional ways. This time, instead of Emily's insecurities leading the way, mine were front and center when I had chosen to mingle instead of sitting with Emily and Teri, trying to get to know Christopher better.

The problem was that it's been a week since Emily bared her soul to me and I've thought of little else. And after seven days, I haven't been able to come up with a solution to our dilemma. I was a man, and a construction worker at that, so my mind was driven to fix things; to find solutions for problems. Except, Emily's emotions weren't something 'to fix' and that left me without a clue as to what the fuck to do.

She has spent the last two years feeling like second place and I've spent the last two years letting our relationship evolve from a marriage to more of a roommate situation. Unintentional roommates who occasionally fucked during the week.

God, I was exactly the jerk she accused me of being.

I had no idea how to make her feel certain of what I felt for her, and that was the crux of it all. We lacked emotional trust. I should be able to tell her that she's the only one for me and she should automatically believe me. She shouldn't need tangible proof of my feelings for her. Still, at this point in our marriage, she did, and I didn't know how to give that to her.

Emily believed in how she felt, and as much as it pained me to admit, I didn't blame her. My wife overheard her husband talking about his sexual relationship with another woman...I mean, what the fuck had I been thinking? Within these past few days, I've tried to imagine how I would feel if the situations were reversed, and the imaginary scenario has actually caused my gut to tighten every time I've tried.

I couldn't imagine what it'd do to me if I came across something that made me believe I wasn't Emily's everything, and I didn't care if I wasn't the best husband in the world. I didn't strive to be. However, what I did want was to be the best husband to *Emily*.

I just didn't know how to do that now.

"Hey," she greeted me as she finally reached me.

"Hey," I greeted back. "What happened to Teri and Christopher?" I prayed my voice was steady and casual.

She smiled impishly at me. "He couldn't stand keeping his hands off her anymore, and so he asked me if they could leave."

I slammed my clenched fists into my pockets. "What did you say?"

This time, her smile showed her perfect row of white teeth. "I assured him that he wasn't being rude at all, and I wouldn't be offended if they left."

"Well, knowing Teri, she'll always choose getting fucked by her current boytoy over anything else." I regretted the words as soon as they were out of my mouth.

Emily's face was pure offended shock. "Wow."

"Em, I'm sorry. I...I didn't mean that. Teri..." I trailed off because I really didn't know how to finish the sentence. I've never judged Teri or her life choices because I never saw anything wrong with them. She chose to be single and enjoy a life with no responsibilities unto anyone other than herself. There was no shame in that.

Emily blinked a couple of times, and then went forth to cut me off at the knees. "Maybe she is a whore according to the standards set by a hypocritical society. And maybe she should be more careful with her choices in entertainment. But at least she gets to live her life with the confidence of knowing where she stands. She never gets disappointed or heartbroken when she doesn't get what she was never expecting." Emily shrugged a delicate shoulder. "She's getting laid with no emotional complications or expectations, and that is probably why her sex life is ten times better than mine, Cynthia's, or Jackie's."

The bottom of my stomach dropped out. "Emily, I'm-"

She stopped me, continuing with her assault. "Right now, Teri is letting Christopher do anything he wants to her, and you know why?" She didn't wait for me to answer. "Because all she has to do is trust him with her body. Her mind, heart, and soul are safely tucked away." Emily's heartbreaking face was full of so much resentment that I almost flinched. She didn't start to walk away from me until she delivered her final blow. "She was always the smartest out of all of us." Emily had never looked so serious when she went to put me in check. "Don't ever speak badly about *any* of my friends again, Marcus."

I stood in shame as I watched Emily walk over and play hostess to a couple of my employees that she knew. I couldn't believe I had said that about Teri, especially when I didn't mean any of it. I liked Teri. She was a great person who, as far as I knew, never did anyone any harm.

This shit with Emily needed to be resolved soon. We were both saying shit that we didn't mean and acting like insecure seventh graders.

"Hey, Marcus," came a voice I didn't need to hear right now.

I turned around. "Hey, Rebecca. Are you having a good time?" I wanted so badly to run after Emily, but with all my employees around, I couldn't risk it. We didn't need to be the source of office and site gossip on Monday.

Really quickly, Rebecca glanced over at where Emily stood before returning her attention to me. "I'm having a great time. So is Malory. She's glad she came."

I did my best to smile and focus on our conversation. "Well, good. I'm glad you are both enjoying yourselves."

"So…is there trouble in paradise," she asked with a small smirk on her face.

She's a woman, she's a woman, she's a woman.

"I'm sorry, Rebecca, I don't know what you mean," I responded with as much civility as I could.

She quickly put on an innocent air. "Oh, it just looked like Emily was upset there for a second."

I turned and dumped the beer I had in my hand in the trash can near the barbecue pit, hoping those few precious seconds would ground me somehow. I really, really needed to call my brother and apologize. I looked back at Rebecca's smug expression. "There's never been any trouble between me and Emily, Rebecca, and there never will be." Her face faltered for a second as I continued. "Let me make something very clear. I try my best to maintain a friendly, open-door relationship with all my employees, you included. However, my wife and my marriage are *no one's* business, Rebecca. If you ever make an assumption about my wife or my marriage again, we're going to have a problem. Do you understand?"

Her face paled as she tried to backtrack. "Oh, Mr. Maxwell…I was just-"

I raised my palm up to stop her. "I don't care what you were 'just', Rebecca. Do you understand?"

"Yes, sir," she mumbled a bit embarrassed.

"Good. Now, please, continue to enjoy the party." She went to walk away before my next words made her pause. "And, Rebecca, one other thing I'd like to make clear. I adore my wife and that's the reason there is never trouble in paradise in regard to our marriage. I would walk onto oncoming traffic if she asked me to." I left her standing there as I took off in search of Kathy Veneble, my H.R. Manager. She needed to be aware of the conversation as quickly as possible.

I finally found Kathy and she was drinking a couple of the guys under the table. Even in the middle of all this crap with Emily, I was happy that my employees were having a good time. "Hey, Kathy, you got a sec?"

She smiled and started waving at me like we hadn't just seen each other yesterday. God, I hoped she wasn't too drunk to talk shop with. Maybe I should wait until Monday.

"Of course, Boss!" she shouted as she made her way over to me.

I searched her face, and she didn't appear to be drunk, but I knew she could hold her booze. "Are you drunk?"

Kathy snorted. "Pfft, please." She threw her thumb back towards the guys. "Drinking with these children, no way. I swear, Marcus, society is making men more, and more weaker by the second."

I laughed and didn't necessarily disagree with her assessment. "I need to talk to you about something really quick."

She must have sensed my seriousness because she morphed into all business. "Shoot."

"Rebecca approached me asking me if there were problems in my marriage," I began.

"*She what?*" she almost sputtered. "Tell me you're kidding?" She definitely looked sober now.

I shook my head. "No." I proceeded to recite the conversation to her. "I just thought you should know in case she didn't understand."

Kathy shook her head, and her face was filled with regret. "I'm sorry, Marcus. I should have taken care of this way earlier."

I could feel myself tense. "What do you mean?"

She let out a deep breath. "A couple of months ago, I overheard her on the phone talking to someone about you." Kathy grimaced. "She was telling the person on the phone how hot she thought you were and that is was a shame you were married, yadda, yadda, yadda." She waved her hand about. "You know all that standard shit women say when they got the hots for someone. I had never seen her act inappropriately towards you, so I thought it was just a harmless crush."

"Well, harmless or not, she needs to get those ideas out of her head." I knew my voice conveyed my annoyance with the situation.

"You're right," she immediately agreed. "Do you want me to speak with her on Monday in a more formal capacity?"

"Yes, please," I answered. "I won't have anyone commenting on my wife in any negative way and that includes making suggestive comments about me."

Kathy nodded her head in understanding. "Of course. I'll handle it, Marcus."

I just nodded and went in search of Emily. I wanted to find her before Rebecca took leave of all her senses and approached her.

I found her walking from the concession stand and hurried to reach her. "Hey?"

She looked up from her phone. "Hey."

"Are you still upset with me?" *Christ, I sounded like a five-year-old.*

Emily tilted her head and peered into my eyes, cutting me to the quick. "I don't know what I feel about you, Marcus."

"Come on, Chill. You know I love Teri, Cynthia, and Jackie to death. I didn't mean to sound like I was judging Teri." She just stood there staring into my eyes and it scared me to death.

She finally spoke. "Then where did that come from?"

"You seemed to like Christopher a little too much for my liking," I answered honestly.

Emily let out a small, sad huff. "How pathetic that I'm jealous over what they have." She shook her head looking confused. "They have no love between them, but they seem happier than two people who have been married for fifteen years."

She said that Teri and Christopher seemed happier than two people who have been married for years, *not* two people who are in love. In that one sentence, I felt like I was losing her.

I couldn't lose her.

There's no way I'd survive in life without her.

"Chill, we're not unhappy," I insisted. "We don't have an unhappy marriage. We're just-"

"Marcus! Emily!"

We both turned to find Brad Henley and his wife making their way towards us. Brad reached out to shake my hand as soon as they approached. "Another successful company barbecue, I see."

"Hey, Brad." I looked at his wife. "Hello, Hope, it's lovely to see you again." I reached out to shake her hand, too.

Brad turned his attention to Emily. "Emily Maxwell, I swear you get prettier and prettier every time I see you."

Emily smiled at him as she looked at Hope. "I swear, Hope, how do you put up with his storytelling?"

Hope laughed good-naturedly. "It's a challenge, for sure. However, this time, he's not telling stories, darling. As always, you are a vision." She leaned in, so she could kiss Emily on the cheek.

Brad had been my boss when I had first gone into construction, and essentially had taught me almost everything I knew about the construction business. In addition, he's been a constant support to me all these years later. I invited him and his wife to every event that was Maxwell Construction related.

"Well, we're going to go get some grub and I'm going to plow the missus with booze, so I can take advantage of her later," Brad joked.

Hope laughed as she went along with the joke. "I keep telling him he doesn't have to ply me with alcohol if he would just wash a dish or do laundry every now and again."

We all laughed as Brad started steering Hope towards the food. "Well, we'll leave you guys to your hosting duties. We'll catch up later," Brad promised.

"We'll see you guys later," I agreed as Emily stood silently next to me. After a few seconds, I turned to her. "Em-"

She turned to me and cut me off. "Marcus, how about we table our problems for right now. We're in the middle of your company barbecue and we are not going to solve anything talking in between socializing with-"

"*My* company barbecue?" I interrupted trying to keep my voice leveled.

She blinked a couple of times before answering, "Well, yeah. I didn't have anything to do with building Maxwell Construction. That was all you."

"That was all me, huh? You had nothing to do with it?"

"Marcus, you're the one who put in all the hours to be where you are today," she reasoned.

Enough was enough.

"Fuck Maxwell Construction," I hissed.

CHAPTER 10

Emily ~

I couldn't contain my shock. Marcus was losing his mind. "Wh...what?"

Marcus's head swiveled around frantically until his gaze settled on the park restrooms. He grabbed me by my hand and would have been, literally, dragging me off towards that direction if I hadn't had the grace to pick up my pace and make it look like I was going with him voluntarily.

The park's restrooms were very neat and clean, probably due to it being a privately owned and operated park, and there were four men's and four women's separated rooms to prevent lines. Incredulousness had me speechless when Marcus pulled me into one of the men's restrooms. "Marcus!"

He had me up against the wall with his palms slapped on either side of my head, caging me in. His grey eyes so heated that they looked like melted silver. "Let's get one thing straight here, Emily. *I* didn't build Maxwell Construction on my own," he stated forcefully.

"Mar-"

"Maxwell Construction exists because of *you*. Everything I do and everything I've done is to provide for you and make you proud of me. So, *without you,* there would be no Maxwell Construction. Since the day I met you, I have never done anything on my own because I live for *you*. I know you don't believe me, but whether you do or not, it doesn't change the fact that you are at the heart of everything I do and all that I am today. Do not *ever* separate yourself from my life like that again," Marcus snapped.

I had no response. I could only look at him, wondering how we got here. Marcus and I didn't fight like this. We didn't have...doubts. We didn't hurt each other.

Well, at least, we never used to.

"Marcus-" I began before he cut me off.

He moved his hands to cradle my face, his thumbs caressing my jaw.

"Jesus, Chill, I don't know how to make you see how much-" Marcus didn't finish his sentence. Instead, he slammed his lips down on mine and I opened my mouth to his invasion, kissing him back with all my feelings of confusion and longing.

Marcus started nipping and trailing kisses down my neck, and I threw my head back to give him more access. My hands got lost in his hair and I closed my eyes, realizing how much I missed this.

How much I missed the feeling of him.

I wanted Marcus so badly, but one of us had to stop this crazy train. We were at a company function. Kathy would freak if she knew we were in here acting like crazed, hormonal teenagers. "Marcus, the barb-"

I felt his teeth sink into my neck before his tongue swiped at the sting. "I don't give a fuck about the barbecue, Chill, or any one person out there." He took one of my tits in his hand and squeezed. "I don't care about anything but slamming my cock deep inside your sweet pussy, baby."

Oh, God.

I supposed this was the part where responsible, respectable Emily would stop him and remind him of his image as the head of the company, but my lady bits were so starved for this kind of passion that they shut responsibility and respectability down with a quickness. I removed my hands from his hair and started to get to work on his belt.

Marcus let out a deep, rugged growl as soon as he realized what I was doing. I'd be lying if I didn't say a part of me wanted to walk out of here and rub it in Rebecca Stalt's face that I had just been had by my husband. I've always known she had a thing for him because, in all honesty, she couldn't hide the expression on her face every time she was around him. However, I knew Marcus would never be interested in her for the simple fact that she was his employee if nothing else.

I finally managed to get through all of Marcus' clothing obstacles, then found my hand wrapped around his hard, warm steel. I could feel myself getting soaked, and so far, all Marcus has done is kiss my neck and grab my tit.

I was such a sucker for my husband.

"God, Chill, I love when you play with my cock like that," Marcus confessed.

He wasn't the only one. Marcus' cock was such a production of perfection that I actually *craved* sucking his dick. I craved so much and desired even more from him that I've never shared with him. In all fairness, my issues with our lack of intimacy were more my inability to voice my desires without being judged than a few drunken memories I'd overheard one night.

I needed to quit being intimidated by my husband.

"Marcus, I need you," I breathed heavily.

He was still kissing my neck when I felt him reach for the bottom of my skirt and start hiking it up. "What do you need from me, baby?"

"Just you, Marcus," I begged.

He nipped my collarbone. "Nu uh, Chill. You gotta tell me what you want me to do to you."

This wasn't new. Marcus has always let me lead in the bedroom. He never pushed or took me beyond my comfort zone, and while I really, really appreciated his concern for my feelings like that, my comfort zone was actually a lot bigger than he realized.

Maybe it was time to clue him in.

I could hear the tearing of fabric alerting me to the demise of my panties. A second later, I could feel Marcus' fingers sliding through my wetness. I let go of his dick and brought his face back to mine. Go big or go home, right? Looking into his perfect face with his burning gaze, I decided to be completely honest in this moment. "I want you to do whatever it is you want to do to me, Marcus." I saw the muscle in his jaw tick, and it made me flood his fingers. I leaned into his ear and whispered, "I want you to fuck me like you just paid for the rights to my body."

He threw his head back and let out the hottest sound I'd ever heard. It was a cross between a laugh and a moan. He took my face in one hand while he expertly played with my pussy with the other. This time, he leaned into my ear and whispered, "I've got news for you, Chill. I *do* own the rights to your body. There's no pretending about it." I felt like my body was going to burst into flames from his words. "From the top of your head to the tips of your toes, I own it all, baby."

I threw my head back as he sank two fingers into my pussy, finally filling me. "Hmm, Marcus…"

Marcus tilted my head, so that I was facing him again. "Look at me, Chill." My eyes fluttered open, and I did my best to maintain eye contact, but his fingers were driving me crazy. "Mean what you say and say what you mean, baby, because if you tell me that I can do whatever I want to you, then this isn't going to end until you're dripping from head to toe in my cum and I've fucked your mouth, your pussy, *and* your ass."

I could feel myself clamp down on his fingers at his dirty words. "All that in the park restroom?"

He let out a small chuckle. "Okay, maybe not all of that here, right now. But Emily…God, if you're serious…" Marcus looked at me like he was afraid I was going to take my words back.

I wasn't.

I knew Marcus was taking responsibility for the part he played in of where we were now and now it was my turn. I needed to quit envying my husband's fifteen-year-old memories and start trying to replace those memories with thoughts of only me. "Marcus, right now, right here, I just need you to fuck me." I leaned forward and nipped his bottom lip. "I promise when we get home tonight, I'll let you do whatever you want to my body, and I won't say no to any of it."

He held me in his silver gaze. "What if I want-"

I stopped him. *"Whatever* you want, Marcus. I...I trust you."

Marcus closed his eyes like he was in pain. When he opened them, I could see so much regret reflected back at me. "No, you don't, Chill. But I swear I'm going to do everything I can to change that."

I gave him a small smile. "Well, you can start by believing me when I tell you I will welcome anything you want to do to me, Marcus."

He let out a groan, and before I knew it, he thrust his cock inside me, replacing his fingers. I wrapped my legs around his waist, and I couldn't hold back. "Oh, God, Marcus," I moaned, not caring if anyone outside could hear me.

"God can't help you, baby," Marcus informed me as he started crashing into me. "Especially, now that I know you want me to fuck you like you're my own personal whore."

"Jesus, Marcus," I breathed.

Marcus hands dug into my thighs, holding me up and against the restroom wall. His face was in the crook of my neck, licking, tasting, and teasing. "That's what you want, isn't it? You want to stop being seen as my sweet, loving wife in the bedroom, right?" I let out a wanton moan, too timid to say yes. "Be clear with me, Emily," he demanded between grunts and thrusts.

It was hard for me to articulate real words, though. Marcus was fucking me hard and rough, and his filthy suggestions had me already on the edge of my orgasm. I always felt full and stretched whenever Marcus was inside me, but this time, he didn't give me time to acclimate myself to his size, so I was having a hard time taking him, even though I was soaked.

And it felt glorious.

The discomfort felt like I was finally get well and truly fucked.

"Emily..." Marcus was waiting for my confirmation.

"Marcus...oh, God...don't stop...I'm going to cum," I begged him.

He stopped his movements, and holding me up, kept me impaled on his cock. "No," he growled. "You don't get to cum until you tell me what you really want. I want the words, Chill."

I opened my eyes and stared into the strained face of my gorgeous husband. I needed to cum so badly that I'd tell him whatever he wanted to know in this moment. "I don't want us to be scared anymore, Marcus. I...I don't want us to be worried about being judged. I want you to fuck me like...like..." *God, why was this so hard?*

Marcus pushed himself up a little further, making me moan again. "You want me to fuck you like what, Em?"

"I want you to use my body like I'm your paid whore. I just don't want you to think I am one," I whispered insecurely.

"Emily," he groaned and started moving again. He didn't say anything further as he sped up and began jackhammering his cock into my pussy so hard that I could feel the wall scraping my back.

I didn't stop him, though.

This was what I wanted.

This was what I've been craving.

I wanted my husband so out-of-control desperate for me that his only thoughts were of making me cum all over him. That's what I wanted and that's what he was delivering right now.

"I'm not going to last much longer, baby. I need you with me. Tell me what you need to take you over the edge with me," Marcus ordered.

I knew exactly what it would take.

I wrapped my arms around his neck, running my hands through his hair as I begged in his ear, "Tell me the first new thing you're going to do to me tonight, Marcus."

I didn't think he could increase his tempo any more than the pace he was already at, but he started slamming into me so hard that I almost screamed at him to pull back; this was nine inches of dick we're talking about here.

But I didn't.

I wanted the animal that he kept caged up out and hungry.

"I'm going to cum all over your perfect fucking face, Chill," Marcus informed me. "I'm going to make you swallow my cock until you can't breathe, and tears are streaming down your beautiful face. Then I'm going to cover it with everything you pull out of me."

His words were so dirty and hot that I let out a scream that was sure to let everyone know outside what we were doing-if they didn't already know-and let my orgasm shake my entire body.

"Goddamn it, Emily," Marcus thundered right before I felt him thicken and erupt inside me. Still, we were desperate for this to continue. My body kept pulsing around him, and he kept pushing inside me until I started to relax, and his cock started to soften.

It was the best fuck he's given me in years.

I wanted to stay in this restroom with him forever. However, I knew I couldn't. "Marcus, we need to...*oh, God...*" I trailed off as I realized we were going to have to go out and face all those people, regardless of the bravery in my head earlier.

Marcus started chuckling as he pulled out and put himself back together. I stood there, still trying to get my bearings, but then Marcus smiled as he began putting me back together, too.

He took my face in his hands once he was done. "Emily, we're going to walk out there like a husband and wife who still crave each other after fifteen years of marriage. We are not going to be embarrassed or ashamed. We are going to own it and make every single person out there green with envy and leave them swimming in jealousy."

I looked into his eyes, and for the first time in a long time, I felt like we were in the marriage I always wanted us to be in. I nodded. "Okay...but...uhm, Marcus?"

"Yeah, baby?"

No panties were going to be an issue. "Your cum is dripping down my thighs," I murmured.

I could see his pupils dilate. "No problem." He lowered himself on his haunches and used his right hand to rub his seed into the skin of my inner thighs. He walked over to the sink, washed his hands, and then held out his hand for me to take. "Ready?"

Holy fuck, was I ever.

CHAPTER 11

Marcus ~
We were finally heading home after helping clean up and put everything away from the barbecue, and it had been the most torturous six hours of my life.

After Emily and I had come out of the restroom, it had been all I could do to hold a reasonably intelligent conversation with anyone.

All I could think about was how hot that restroom fuck had been and how I was going to ruin her mind and body with all the sick, twisted, filthy things I wanted to do to her when we got home.

Well, in my mind the things I wanted to do to her weren't all that sick, twisted, or filthy in comparison to some of the shit people were into these days, but to do the things I wanted to do to my sweet wife, all my fantasies felt sick, twisted, and filthy.

When we had emerged from the restroom, it was obvious from all the knowing glances that almost everyone there had known that I'd had just had sex with my wife in the men's park restroom. However, instead of feeling dishonored or inappropriate, I had gathered Emily in my arms and kissed her all over her face until she was laughing with me. I loved Maxwell Construction and all the people who worked for me, but as loyal as they all were, and as long as some of them have worked for me, still, none of them matter to me more than Emily. So, when it came between what they thought of me having sex with my wife at the company barbecue and pleasing Emily, it was no contest.

I'll always pick being balls-deep in Emily over doing anything else.

Always.

We had spent the rest of the barbecue playing host and hostess, and if anyone had any negative opinions about what we had done, no one had said anything or acted differently towards us. I personally believed they all wished they could have been us.

I'd had a good time and I think Emily had one, too. However, that still hadn't stopped me from wanting to leave the barbecue right out and disappear with her as soon as we had exited that restroom.

Like I said, the most torturous six hours of my life.

Now we were heading home, and my dick kept twitching in anticipation of what the rest of the night was going to bring. I just prayed that she meant what she said, and she wasn't just trying to change things up because we were having issues.

When Emily had told me that she wanted me to fuck her like a whore but didn't want me to think she actually was one, it had broken my heart a little. She actually thought I'd judge her or her desires, and I would never do that. And because I would never share Emily with *anyone*, as long as she didn't want to bring another man or woman into the bedroom with us, I was open to anything she wanted to try.

Well...anything with the exception of her dressed up in spiked leather, wearing a strap on.

We'd have to sit down and have a long talk if that scenario ever came up.

Luckily for me, I was pretty confident that wasn't Emily's niche. She said she wanted me to fuck her like a hot piece of paid ass. That meant she wanted to be used by me and not the other way around. My biggest concern about all this was the morning after. I wanted her to wake up tomorrow morning feeling thoroughly fucked and used, but feeling confident and sexy, too. I didn't want her waking up feeling doubtful or embarrassed.

I wanted her to wake up knowing just how far gone I was for her.

We pulled up to the house and I could see her fidgeting with her skirt as I coasted the car up the driveway while the garage door was opening to let us in. I wanted to calm her, but I wasn't sure how to go about that. All I knew was that if she changed her mind-and I would totally respect that-there was a very good chance I would lose my mind if she did.

She'd have to commit me and all I could hope for was that my future chess-playing partner didn't pee on himself during our chess games.

The garage door closed behind us, and I silently got out of the car and walked over to open Emily's door for her. That was one of the few things I wouldn't compromise on. I understood that we've come a long way as a society from the 1800s, but no matter Emily's strengths and capabilities, I will always open her doors for her, stand until she sits, and carry anything heavy for her.

I was a firm believer in the fact that, yes, women were capable of doing anything that men could do, but they shouldn't have to. As a man, it was my job to help support Emily in being the best version of herself that she can be. However, at the same time, making sure she didn't have to do it all by herself.

During this past week, I've been made very aware that I have failed miserably at that, and I was going to do all I could to rectify my mistakes. Plus, being a man, it was a win for me that she wanted to let me start making it right in the bedroom.

Emily got out of the car, and she wouldn't look at me as she adjusted the strap of her purse over her shoulder. She walked around me, then stood by the door into the house as she waited for me to unlock the door and let her in.

I followed in behind her, and I wondered how she could let me fuck her in the park restroom, surrounded by people, but be nervous alone with me at home.

Emily walked straight through the kitchen and living room to head towards our bedroom. She hadn't uttered word since we said our farewells to the park staff after cleaning up. I had no idea what she was thinking, and then a paranoid thought had me running after her.

This time, I will *break down the bathroom door if she's locked herself in there again.*

Emily wasn't locked inside the bathroom when I made it to our bedroom, though. She was actually standing in the middle of the room, seemingly waiting for me. I stood in the doorway just staring at her. Her beauty was enough to cut a man off at the knees.

Emily was my greatest strength and my strongest weakness.

When she finally spoke, she almost did bring me to my knees. "So, do I drop to my knees in front of you like a good, little whore or do you want to wrap my hair around your fist and force me to my knees like a bad, little whore?" Emily's green eyes never wavered from my gray ones as her voice got huskier. "What do you need me to be for you, Marcus?"

I couldn't speak right away because I was feeling too many things.

First, my dick was rock fucking hard just hearing those filthy words coming out of Emily's mouth. Beautiful, sweet-looking women didn't talk like that, and the contrast had my dick trying to push out of my pants. Second, I just needed her to be her, and I was irritated that she still didn't know that. Third, I was man enough to admit I was feeling a bit apprehensive.

After fifteen years of marriage, Emily was finally opening up and trusting me to fulfill her deepest, dirtiest sexual fantasies, what if I disappointed her?

Fuck.

Only a man would understand my trepidation. No matter how much women would love for us men to work off emotions and understanding, we just didn't. We were conquerors, and we were competitors, and that part would always drive us in the bedroom. I had an animalistic need to be the best fuck Emily has ever had and to make sure she never questioned it again.

I slowed stalked towards her. "Since all I need is for you to be you, I think you need to tell me what it is you need from me, not the other way around, Chill."

I could see her breathing pick up and a flush working up her neck. "I...I..."

There was no way I was going to let her lose ground now. "Here's the thing, Em. It doesn't matter which you choose because I have every intention of fucking all versions of you by the time morning comes." I took her face in my hand and rubbing my thumb across her bottom lip asked. "Tell me what you really want, Emily."

She looked at me with such naked honesty in her eyes that I knew her words were true and real. "I want you to want me so badly that you can't hold back. I want you to really embrace the knowledge that I really, really won't say no to anything that you want to do to me." Emily ran her hands up my chest over my shirt. "I don't care if it's sweet and loving or degrading and violent. I just want you out of control."

Holy Mary, Mother of God.

My arm shot out and I wrapped a chuck of her chocolate waves around my fist, then I pushed her down onto her knees in front of me. The rush was better than any shot of heroin could ever be. My wife, the woman I loved, was willing to let me fuck her as dirty and as filthy as I wanted, and I felt high off the realization.

She looked up at me when her knees met the carpet and I felt viciousness course through my body. "Take my cock out, Em," I instructed her while I maintained my grip in her hair.

Emily went for my belt and had my pants lowered and my dick out in record time. She started running her wrapped hand up and down my shaft in anticipation of what I was going to say or do next. And God help me when she lifted her green gaze back up at me, waiting her instructions.

Fuck, she was going to be the death of me.

I stared down at her, and in all honesty, I just wanted to grab her, throw her on the bed, then just get to fucking the shit out of her, but this was all about her not me.

God, I was such a sorry sap. The tip of my dick was already leaking with the knowledge that I was going to spray my load all over the stunning face looking up at me right now.

Damn, but I was a lucky motherfucker.

I reached down with my left hand and took hold of the base of my dick, forcing her to let go. "Place your hands on my thighs, Chill." She immediately and eagerly complied. "Now open up for me, baby. Let me see those soft, pink lips wrapped around my cock," I instructed as I softy slapped her full, bottom lip with the head of my dick.

Emily licked her pretty lips, and as soon as she opened her mouth wide enough, I plunged my cock down her throat, and I swear, I almost shot my load right then and there.

She immediately gagged, but she didn't push me away and I genuinely worried that I was going to embarrass myself during our first time together like this. My body was tense, and I was on edge.

Emily always gave epic blowjobs. She always sucked my dick like it was her favorite thing in the world to do. However, now that she was adding that skill to letting me fuck her throat...well, let's just say, every second that I lasted was an appreciated miracle.

I pulled back a little before pushing back in, and when she gagged this time, she looked up at me and confidently showed me the tears leaking down the sides of her face.

I lost my shit.

I tightened my hold in her hair and started fucking her sweet, hot mouth. "Fuck, yeah, Chill," I groaned as I sped up my pace and increased the depth. And, God bless her, she didn't stop me.

Emily kept her hands on my thighs and the only sign she gave of a struggle was when she would clench her hands around my thigh muscles when my cock pummeled the back of her throat. Other than that, she let me fuck her mouth like I was fucking her pussy, and the little sounds that would escape when I gave her a chance to breathe suggested that she was loving it.

Even though she held all the power here, I wanted to give her something back while she continued to suck and swallow, bringing me to the brink. I wanted her so turned on that she'd agree to anything I wanted. Luckily, I've recently learned what it took to help get her there.

I took my other hand, and wrapping it in her hair, I held her head as if it were her hips and kept right on fucking her face. "That's it, baby, suck my fucking cock. Swallow it all the way down, Chill." I could see her closing her eyes, and I swear, she looked like she was on the verge of cumming herself. I pulled my cock all the way out of her mouth and tapped her lips with it. "You like sucking my dick, baby?"

Emily's gaze shot up towards mine and the heat in them pushed me to the brink of real insanity. "Yes," she panted.

"Do you wish you could wrap your pretty lips around my dick every day?" I taunted. I knew I was going to cum soon, so I wanted her to be just as satisfied by this experience as I was, no doubt, going to be.

"Yes, Marcus," she whimpered.

I rammed my cock back into her mouth and it wasn't a minute later I was feeling the tingles gathering at the base of my balls and I was warning her, "I'm going to cum, Chill."

Emily's hands left their place on my thighs, and she grabbed the base of my dick, pumping my cock to help me along. I tangled my left hand tighter in her hair while I grabbed my cock with my right hand, and I pulled out of the paradise that was her mouth with perfect timing.

Emily didn't close her eyes. She didn't even flinch when the first rope of my hot cum hit her cheek. She locked me with her stare as I pulled on my dick, aiming my load all over her cheeks, lips, and chin. I wasn't sure how long I came, but by the time I was done, Emily's face and neck were a perfect picture of creamy white stickiness.

I stared down at my wife, and she was breathing so heavily that you would have thought she'd just run a marathon. She was panting and flushed, and even fully clothed, she looked hotter than any naked woman I've ever seen.

As I was coming down off my high, the thought of taking her picture crossed my mind. I released my hold on her hair and cradled her face in both my hands. I started rubbing my cum all over her face and I lost my breath at watching her let me dirty her up. "Jesus Christ, Emily," I revered.

"How do I look covered in your cum, Marcus?" she whispered.

"So fucking beautiful that you should be covered in it every fucking damn day," I answered honestly.

CHAPTER 12

Emily ~

I woke up feeling like I'd just been in a car wreck.

My body hurt in places I never even knew existed. My jaw ached and my throat shared its pain as I swallowed. My arms felt like I'd never done a day's worth of physical work in all my life, and my legs felt like they were going to fall off any second now.

However, the greatest ache was the one between my legs.

After Marcus had cum on my face last night, we had undressed and had taken a shower. I didn't mind his cum all over me, but we had fucked in a public restroom earlier, for Christ's sake. A shower was necessary, no matter how clean those restrooms were.

Once we had entered the shower and the hot water had washed him away, he had cleaned every nook and cranny on my body, and then had proceeded to fuck me up against the shower wall. I'd been so worked up from the face fucking, and it had been years since he had fucked me in the shower, I had erupted almost instantly.

Marcus had fucked me through my orgasm, and once I had been able to stand again, he had dried me off, then himself, and then carried me with my arms wrapped around his neck and my legs wrapped around his waist to our bed.

He hadn't hovered over me and kissed me like I thought he was going to. He hadn't kissed or played with my tits. He hadn't bothered with any other part of my body as he had dropped to his knees at the end of the bed, grabbed the back of my thighs, then pushed my legs back and open for what he had wanted to do next.

Before I could ask or protest, Marcus had buried his face in my pussy and was licking, biting, and teasing me into another orgasm. I had cried for how much I missed the blinding pleasure of Marcus tasting and devouring me. Plus, last night had been so much better as he would occasionally break from what he'd been doing to talk dirty to me. My orgasm had finally hit me when he had growled that he wanted to eat my cunt for breakfast every morning.

It seemed that now that Marcus was aware that dirty words were my undoing, he had spent most of the night talking to me like I was a street whore.

And I fucking loved it.

Loved. It.

After he had licked me to orgasm, Marcus had slammed into me and had fucked me like my body had been created for that purpose only. It had been hard, fast, rough, and painful, and I remembered begging him not to ever stop.

That hadn't been the end of it, either. After that round, he had made me ride him until he came, and after more kissing, licking, touching, sucking, and biting, Marcus had put me on all fours and had fucked me from behind until I had passed out from the orgasm.

It was the first time I had ever passed out from multiple orgasms, and it would be something I would never forget.

Ever.

The sex had been messy, dirty, hard, and thorough. It had been the best night of my life, and now my body was paying the price. Still, I'd pay it over, and over again.

The weight of Marcus' arm dropped across my waist as he pulled me back towards his warm, hard chest. "Hey, baby," he nuzzled into the back of my neck.

I wrapped my arm over his and pushed myself back into his warmth. "Good morning."

Marcus was already rubbing his morning wood on my ass. "It's going to be," he promised wickedly.

I snickered as I laid out a test for him. "What if I told you my body was too sore for that?"

I felt his hand travel south and he didn't speak until his fingers were rubbing that special, little nub. "I'd tell you I don't give a shit how sore your pussy is because I can eat your sweet, tight cunt for as long as I have to in order for you to be able to take me." I couldn't contain the moan that escaped my lips as he kept working my clit. "Besides," he continued, "it's a little too late for you to hide the fact that you like it when it hurts." Marcus bit my earlobe. "Or maybe you're denying me that hot, snug cunt of yours, hoping that I'll finally fuck you up that tight, sexy ass of yours, hmm. Is that it, Chill?"

I could feel my body heat from the inside out. That was the one thing we hadn't gotten to last night. We'd been in such a frenzy for each other that there was no way we could have tried to have anal sex without causing serious damage to my body. I knew that I wanted Marcus out of control, but I still had enough sense to know that we needed to take care with that new attempt.

It didn't stop me from backing into him and rubbing against him like a cat in heat, though. For someone who never used to incorporate dirty talk in the bedroom, Marcus was knocking it out of the park with his filthy words and promises.

Marcus went from playing with my clit to dipping one finger into my pussy and spreading my slickness around. I thought he was going to finger fuck me until I was wet enough to take his cock, but he surprised me when he pulled his hand away from my pussy altogether and smeared my wetness around my back puckered hole.

I wish I could say I clenched or jerked forward in shock since he's never played with me there before, but I didn't. I welcomed the taboo act and moaned out his name.

Marcus' voice sounded like he was strangling on his lust. "Fuck me, Chill, is that what you want? Is that what you're hoping for?" He bent his head and bit my shoulder so hard that I let out a cry. "Do you need me to fuck you up the ass, baby? Do you want to finally know how it feels to *really* be fucked like a dirty whore?"

"Marcus," I begged, not exactly sure what I was begging for.

I felt Marcus position himself behind me, but instead of attempting to have anal sex with me, he guided his cock to the entrance of my pussy and rubbed my slit, soaking himself in my cream before he slammed up inside me. *"Marcus…oh, God…"*

"Fuck, yeah. God, Chill," he grunted as he started moving inside me. Marcus pulled me until my back was flushed with his chest and his lips were perfect against my ear. I knew he was going to dirty talk me into another orgasm, and I welcomed it.

My pussy was so sore and swollen that Marcus' dick felt so much bigger than usual-if that was even possible-but it still felt divine. I never understood the concept of how pain could feel good before, but I understood it now. The discomfort I was feeling was real, but the idea that I wanted my husband so much that I didn't care about the pain had me soaking wet. I imagined it compared to how athletes trained and trained, then pushed themselves beyond the pain because their ultimate goal was worth all they had to go through to get there.

That was how much I craved Marcus. I desired him so much that the pain and discomfort my body may have had to experience at the hands of whatever he chose to do to me was so worth it.

"Don't worry, Emily," Marcus assured me. "I have every intention of bending you over and drilling your virgin ass with my nine-inch cock."

"Oh, God," I mewled, his words working me into a quivering mass of heat.

He was working his cock deeper and harder into me as he laid out promise after filthy promise. "Believe me when I tell you I plan on working you so good that you'll be begging me to fuck you in the ass every time I bend you over, baby."

Without warning, my pussy clamped down like a vise and my entire body was trembling with an orgasm so intense that there were white spots dancing behind my eyes.

"Fuck." Marcus thundered in my ear as he came inside me.

We laid there afterwards, the harshness of our breathing the only sound in the room. Jesus, what was it about dirty talk that was so damn hot?

I raised my arms over my head and pointed out my toes until I was stretching my entire body in a very satisfied weariness. "You're very good at that, you know."

Laughing, Marcus rolled onto his back. "What? Fucking you?"

I smiled. "Well, that, too. However, I was referring to your gift for dirty talk."

Marcus was so quiet that I turned my head to look over at him. He was on his back, and he was looking up at the ceiling. His face looked so serious, and his voice lacked all mirth when he spoke. "I was always afraid of offending or insulting you." Marcus let out a deep breath. "I thought…I don't know what I thought."

I disagreed. He knew. He probably just didn't know how to put it into words that wouldn't cause a fight right now, was my bet. Still, I didn't push him. I knew that great sex wasn't going to make our issues go away just like that. I also knew that we needed to find our way back to actively loving each other instead of being just two people who lived together.

"Hey," I said, deciding to try and lighten the mood. "Why don't we call Matt and ask him and Sandra if we can steal the kids for the day? We haven't kidnapped them in a while."

Mercifully, Marcus jumped onboard. "Where do you want to take them?"

"How about the trampoline place in town? They had lots of fun the last time we took them."

He let out a groan. "Are you up to jumping on a trampoline? I gotta tell you, Chill, this pushing forty is rough."

I laughed as I sat up. "I don't think it's our age, Marcus. I think we just need to exercise more." I looked back at him and gave him a wink.

He tried to reach for me, but I was quicker making my escape off the bed. "Oh, I definitely think we need to exercise more. I think we should exercise every day and three times on the weekend." I laughed all the way to the bathroom.

After I took care of business, I brushed my teeth, then jumped in the shower. I was reaching for the shampoo when I heard the shower door open. I couldn't help but start laughing at the memory of the last time Marcus had joined me in here.

"What's so funny?"

I stepped back to make more room for him." I was just thinking of the last time you came in her with me."

He snorted a smirk. "The last time I came in here with you, you came, too, if I recall."

Marcus grabbed the shampoo before I could, and I knew he was going to wash my hair again. "I was talking about last week. You know, I really am sorry I knocked you on your ass, Marcus." He turned me around and started washing my hair. "In my defense, you should have warned me that you were planning on kissing your way down my body."

"The fact that I needed to warn you just proves how much of an idiot I've been," he retorted.

I closed my eyes and let myself enjoy his machinations. "We've both been idiots."

He grunted in a silent agreement. I continued to let him wash me in silence and it felt glorious. I had every intention of returning the favor with throwing a bonus blowjob into the mix. I was thinking of how maybe I'll ask him to cum all over me again when his wandering finger jolted me out of my musings. I opened one eye. "Whatcha doing with that finger, Mister?"

One of his perfectly arched black brows lifted as he rubbed the tip of his soapy, wet finger over my ass opening. "If you need to ask, I'm doing it wrong."

"Marcus…"

His voice was rough with lust, but serious when he looked down at me. "I really want in there, Chill. The only reason I didn't do it last night was because, no matter how many times I came fucking you, I still couldn't work the edge off." He kept swirling his finger around and I could feel my body start to flush. "If you hadn't passed out on me, I probably could have gone a couple of more rounds. That's how starved I was for you." Marcus smirked. "Hell, I'm still starved for you. However, I would never want to truly hurt you, no matter how dark our fantasies go." He quit playing with my ass, and instead, lifted me, causing me to wrap my legs around his waist. He had my back against the tiled wall and his cock inside me before I could even get a good grip on him.

I did my best to hold on as he nuzzled his face in my neck and began pounding into me. "God, yes," I moaned.

"I can't take your ass until I buy some lube and whatever I might need to take care of you afterwards," he informed me in between thrusts.

It was almost comical how the topic of anal sex could be so crude and taboo, yet Marcus spoke about it as if it were part of love making. His plan was to fuck me in the ass like I was a dirty slut, but still take care of any of my discomforts afterwards as if I was a delicate flower. What a contradiction.

He continued as if reading my mind. "Don't get me wrong, Chill. Once I get my cock inside that tight ass of yours, I'm going slam my cock inside you like a battering ram. I'm going to make you beg me to stop." I could already feel the telltale signs of an orgasm as he painted his picture of our first time. "But I'm going to make sure you're taken care of afterwards, baby." I could feel his smile against my neck. "Besides, I need you to be able to do it again, and again, and again." I let out a strained laugh.

God, how I loved this man.

That thought stayed in my head as Marcus brought me to orgasm. It stayed with me as he washed me again. It stayed with me as I washed him. And it stayed with me as we got dressed and he called Matt.

I was throwing my hair up when I stopped to really take a look at my reflection in the mirror. I wasn't ugly by any means, but while I needed to embrace that I wasn't twenty-seven anymore, I also wasn't eighty-seven.

I was thirty-seven with no children and a routine career. There was no reason I couldn't go to the gym and tighten some shit up. There was no reason I couldn't wake up a little bit earlier and style my hair.

Marcus has never made a comment about my looks or appearance, so I knew he didn't really care overly much, but improvements couldn't hurt. I wanted to feel desired above anyone else in his eyes, so maybe it was time I put some effort to feeling the part instead of just useless wishing.

CHAPTER 13

Marcus ~

It was Sunday evening and Emily was sitting across from me as we ate dinner. She was just sitting there, minding her own goddamn business, and all I could think about was how I was going to find an adult store this week and buy everything I needed to finally be able to sink into her ass this coming weekend.

As I thought about it, maybe we could take an overnight trip somewhere. We haven't done that in ages. Hell, we haven't done a lot of stuff together in ages. One of the perks to never having had children was that we were supposed to be fancy free and be able to live in the moment. There was nothing stopping me from dragging Emily across the dining table right now and just start fucking her. A no-kid perk, for sure.

We had a lot of catching up to do.

"What does your week look like?"

She looked up at me. "There's a new client Melissa and I are meeting with on Wednesday, but other than that, it's business as usual. Oh," she continued, smiling mischievously at me, "we do have a client who's coming in on Tuesday to dispute some pricing."

"What time? I think I can carve out some time in my day to watch," I told her.

Emily was gleeful. "I know, right?" She shook her head. "Some people just don't know."

Melissa Swan was a shark. A very rich, successful, independent, ferocious shark. According to Em, Melissa's contracts were ironclad, and she had a brain that could calculate numbers and measurements on the drop of a dime. The woman never forgot what was said in negotiations. Why Swan Interior Designs wasn't a bigger player in the field, I had no idea.

"Who's the new client?"

She shrugged a shoulder. "A Gerald Dawson, I do believe. He's some executive of some sort."

I knew Gerald Dawson and he was an epic asshole. He was pampered, privileged, and thought his money entitled him to anything he wanted. "I know who he is."

Surprise flashed across Emily's face. "You do?"

I stabbed my steak with my fork. I didn't want my opinion of him to color how Emily was going to treat him when they met. I mean, I knew Emily would always behave professionally, but she loved her job and the creations she helped design with Melissa, I didn't want to taint any of her experiences. "He works for his father's money marketing firm. I do believe his grandfather started the company and rumor is that his father is looking to retire soon, and Gerald is inheriting a lot of his father's responsibilities." I took a drink of my beer in hopes that it kept my voice smooth and neutral. "He commissioned Maxwell Construction to build a mother-in-law quarters on the south end of his property on Milbourne."

Emily let out a low whistle. "Milbourne. Nice."

She was pulling her fork from her mouth after taking a bite of her steak and images of my cock sliding in and out of that mouth flooded my mind. I shook my brain clear.

I mean, the woman had to eat, nutrients and all that.

"Maybe that's what he wants you guys to decorate," I suggested.

She finished chewing and took a drink of her wine. "Maybe. We'll see on Thursday."

We finished eating in comfortable silence, but it gave me too much time to think about things. I knew things were a little bit better between us after the company barbecue, but I also knew that our issues went deeper than just good sex.

In the real world, people weren't able to spend all their extra time worshipping their spouse, even if they wanted to. It wasn't realistic or healthy. People had to have time for themselves. They needed to be their own person, independent of their spouse. They had to have their own friends, their own hobbies, and their own likes and dislikes.

I needed to make Emily feel confident and secure during those times when I was being independent of her. While Emily was the reason for everything that drove me, she wasn't a part of every second of my every day just like I wasn't hers.

When she was working on a design with Melissa, she wasn't thinking about me. And when I was looking at building plans, I wasn't thinking about her. And that was okay. We didn't need to live in each other's pockets. I just needed to find a way for her to know that my every thought might not be of her, but every breath I took was for her.

We ate in silence for a little while longer before I couldn't take it anymore. "Em, come here."

She looked up from her plate. "What?"

I dropped my silverware onto my plate and pushed my chair back away from the table. "I said, *come here.*"

Emily quietly placed her fork down and regarded me from across the table. "Why?"

I went for complete honesty. "I was going to have you sit on my lap and hold you while I tried to convince you to go up the coast with me or something this weekend, but now I just want you sitting on my lap, so I can finger fuck your pussy as you straddle my cock and push your tits in my face."

Her green gaze widened, and her chest started to rise with excitement. Her lips rolled in between her teeth, and I knew she was unsure about how to respond. Our sex life may have gotten dirtier these past couple of days, but we were still new to the brazenness of our wants. I spent the past fifteen years always treating Emily like a respectable lady. I imagined it was going to take some time for her to get used to me telling her to bend over whenever I got the urge.

I watched as she stood, and then cursed all the heavenly creatures above when I was reminded that she was wearing jeans. She was halfway past the table when I stopped her. "Stop." Emily came to an ungraceful halt, confusion dancing across her lovely face. I leaned back in the chair, resting my laced fingers across my stomach. "I can't very well get my fingers in that sweet slit of yours, Chill, if you're wearing jeans." Her chest started heaving faster as I spoke. "I want you stripped of everything but your bra and panties by the time you make it to me."

I waited in anticipation at what she was going to do. I was quickly learning that Emily's desires exceeded far beyond slow, missionary style and there was nothing I wanted more than to find out exactly how far those boundaries extended.

Emily started slowly stripping out of her shirt, and when it cleared her head, I got a bird's eye view of her glorious tits encased in white lace. She kicked off her sandals and shimmied out of her jeans with each step she took towards me. For a second, I wished I had asked her to come to me completely naked, but staring at her now, wearing only a lace bra and non-matching blue panties, Emily looked hotter than any stripper dancing any pole around the world right now.

I remained silent while she wrapped her arms around my neck as she straddled my lap. She pulled back enough to be face-to-face. "Like this?"

I ran my hands up and over the top of her thighs and around the sides. My hands were splayed across her skin, touching as much of her as I could. I looked into her eager face, and in this moment, I wanted to make it all about her. "Tell me all your secrets, Chill."

She ran her hands down over my shoulders and started tracing my neck. She cleared her throat. "I don't have any secrets, Marcus."

I moved my hands to grip her on either side of her waist, loving the feel of this woman in my arms. Or on my lap, as were the case. "Okay, maybe, you don't have secrets." I leaned in and kissed her along her jawline. "So, then, why don't you tell me what you think about when I'm not home and your fingers are rubbing that hard, little clit of yours."

Emily threw her head back, giving me more access to her jaw and neck. I didn't miss how she slowly started to rub herself back and forth over my hardened cock. "I don't th-"

I bit into her neck, stopping her automatic denial. She yelped as I corrected her. "Don't lie to me, Chill." I stopped kissing her neck and pulled my head up to look at her. "Look at me, Em." She lowered her head and looked into my eyes, her body still rubbing against mine. "I know you want more. I know you crave more than what I've been giving you all these years." Emily looked away as if I were accusing her of some great transgression. "Tell me, baby."

Her eyes were glassy when her eyes returned to mine. "Wh…what if you don't like what I like, Marcus? What if I want something so…dirty that it makes you change the way you feel about me?" And that was what was at the heart of her issues. She still had doubts about what she meant to me.

"Do you want to bring someone else into the mix? Another man or woman?" I hated to ask, but I had to. I just prayed her answer was going to be no.

Shock registered on Emily's face. "Oh, God, no." She shook her head. "Marcus, it would destroy me to see you with another woman, no matter the circumstances and…and I wouldn't even know how to start desiring another man. You've been the center of everything I feel for so long that other men don't even begin to register."

Thank fuck.

I gripped her waist tighter. "Then tell me, baby."

The shyness that came over Emily was so endearing. "I…I just want to try different stuff. There might be things I find I don't like, but I want to try for the things that I will end up liking."

I ran my hands up her back, then back down again. "Like being on your knees while I paint your beautiful face with my cum?"

Emily blushed. "Yeah," she whispered. "Like that."

"With the exception of you bringing someone else into our bedroom, or you wanting to harness on a strap-on and taking on the role of the man, I'll try whatever you want, Chill." I wanted to rid her of all her insecurities. I wanted her trust. I knew I had her love, but, God, how I wanted her trust, too.

She went to play with the buttons on my shirt, and while I wanted her to look at me while she confessed her desires, if she needed to concentrate on the buttons of my shirt, then so be it. "I don't think I want anything too wild or unnatural…" She let out a soft laugh, trying to lighten the moment when we both knew this was a big deal.

"So, then, tell me," I encouraged still moving my hands all over her back, ass, and thighs.

Thank God the house was completely silent or else I was pretty sure I would have been able to hear her with how soft her voice was. "I wonder what it would feel like…oh, God, Marcus…" Emily dropped her head on my shoulder and hid her face from me. I didn't know if it was embarrassment or shame, but I felt myself getting irritated because she should never feel either of those things with me.

I was going to suggest I tell her what I wanted to do to her, but as I thought about it, I realized I didn't want to steer her in this. I wanted to know that everything she let me do was because it was what *she* desired and not because she was giving into me again.

I brought my hand to the back of her neck. "How about after you tell me what you want to try, I'll tell you what I want to try?"

Emily pulled back and looked at me again. She looked so pensive. It was almost as if this moment was going to determine the rest of our marriage. I wanted to reassure her again, but she spoke before I could get a word out. "Have you ever wanted to pull my hair to the point of pain?" she asked.

I could feel heat begin to slither throughout my body. I kept her eyes locked onto mine when I answered, "Yes."

"Have you ever wanted to leave bruises or bite marks…hickeys on my body?"

I swallowed. "Yes."

Emily began rubbing herself across my cock again. "Have you ever wanted to wrap your hand around my throat, holding me down, as you forced yourself inside me as far as you could go?"

I could stop the groan that escaped as the picture she painted took residence inside my head. "More than you know, Chill."

"Have you ever wanted to spank my ass while you were behind me?"

"Yes."

"Have you ever wanted to slap my lips, my cheeks with your cock?" I couldn't believe how hard my dick was at hearing Emily voice her curiosities. It felt like I couldn't breathe. "Have you ever wanted me to ride your face?"

"I dream of it," I confessed.

Emily started upping her tempo. She was flat out dry humping my cock now. "And I already know you want to fuck my ass…" she moaned on a whisper.

I squeezed the fuck out of her hips, and I couldn't stop the next words that left my lips. "I want to do more than fuck your ass, Chill. I want to rip it open."

She threw her head back, then really started rubbing her clit against the hard ridge of my jeans. I nearly blew my load when Emily looked back down at me and moaned, "What I really want to try is for you to fill my pussy with a dildo while you're fucking me deep in my ass, Marcus. I've wondered about double penetration with you."

And just like that, I was so done.

I grabbed her hips and ran her back and forth over me until Emily threw her head back once again, but this time, on the tremor of an orgasm. *"Marcus..."*

Emily was shaking and her skin was covered in goosebumps. Her pussy was soaking my jeans and I was pretty sure I was on the verge of having a heart attack.

After her shuttering subsided, I lifted her in my arms bride-style, then headed towards our bedroom. "Marcus..." she whispered with her face buried in my neck.

I hugged her closer. "I'm going to do all that stuff and more to you, Emily. I swear. But right now, I just want to lay you down and love every inch of your body slowly and thoroughly, baby."

She tightened her hold on me as she conceded, "Okay."

CHAPTER 14

Emily ~

Melissa and I were headed to meet with Gerald Dawson at his home on Milbourne. Marcus' hunch had been correct. Gerald wanted to commission Melissa to design and decorate the additional quarters Maxwell Construction had built on his property.

"So, Dawson is a bit of a dick," Melissa announced from behind the wheel of her white Lexus SUV. "Granted he's a dick who's easy on the eyes, but still a dick, nonetheless."

I laughed. "Thanks for the warning, Liss, but I'm just the note taker. He's going to be dealing with you, not me."

Her snort held all kinds of sarcasm. "You're a lot of things, Emily, but *just* a note taker isn't one of them."

I rolled my eyes. "I know how much you value me, Liss. Still, to the rich and entitled, I'm the hired help. Let's keep it that way."

Melissa shook her head at me. "While I'm thankful for every deal and dollar, I envy you sometimes. Some of these people really fucking suck donkey balls."

I laughed again. "I know. That's why I prefer to keep my head down just taking notes."

"Well, even though I'm the one Dawson's going to be dealing with, he's got a thing for big boobs. You'll definitely be on his radar," Melissa warned as we neared Milbourne Street.

"I'll do my best to act appropriately, ma'am," I vowed.

She snorted again. "Emily, you always act appropriately. I was just warning you, so that if he crosses the line, you're not shocked to shit when I split his face open with my back hand."

I really did let out a deep laugh then. "You really are the best boss ever, Liss."

She nodded in affirmation. "You're damn right, I am."

Melissa turned on Milbourne and the homes that aligned the street could only be owned by the One Percent. If you didn't know better, you'd think you were lost in Beverly Hills.

"This is it," Melissa stated. I looked on in awe was we drove up the circular driveway to stop right in front of a three story...well, mansion.

We gather our stuff, then both got out of Melissa's SUV. I stood by and followed behind her once she started making her way up the front steps. Jesus, were these even called steps? As I looked upon this house, I was boldly reminded of the difference between well-off, rich, and wealthy, and Gerald Dawson was playing on the fringes of wealthy. "Jesus," I muttered.

Melissa knocked on the front door. "Don't let this crap impress you, Em. Remember, all this is a reflection of his grandfather's hard work, not his. His father was able to maintain it, but once he's out of the picture, we'll see just how well good, old Gerald is at the reins."

She had a point. Inherited wealth was not an impressive feat. Hard-earned wealth was where the praise should be directed. "Well, go Granddad."

Melissa laughed as the front door swung open. To my surprise, it wasn't a butler or maid who answered. "Melissa," Gerald welcomed.

"Gerald, how are you?" Melissa turned towards me and made the introductions. "I'd like for you to meet my assistant." She waved a hand between us. "Gerald Dawson, Emily Maxwell. Emily, I'd like you to meet Mr. Gerald Dawson."

I reached my hand out to shake his. He took my hand in his as he cocked his head. "Maxwell, you say? Are you in association with Maxwell Construction?" I opened my mouth to answer, but he continued on to explain why he was asking. "I only ask because the addition you ladies will be looking at today was designed and built by Maxwell Construction."

I couldn't help the smile that took over my face. I was always proud of Marcus, and I never passed up a chance to brag about him. "Marcus Maxwell is my husband," I informed him.

His eyebrows shot up towards his dark blonde hair. "Lucky Marcus," he murmured as he made no bones about looking down my body. However, I was dressed appropriately and professionally, so it wasn't like he was going to get an eyeful of anything.

"Thank you, Mr. Dawson. I'll be sure to remind Marcus tonight when he gets home," I laughed it off, least I offend him before we even got our feet in the door.

Gerald smiled and stepped aside, giving Melissa and I room to enter his home. "Please, come in, ladies. I'm eager to show you the separate quarters."

The inside of Gerald Dawson's house looked like it took a team of twenty housekeepers to keep it shiny clean. I wasn't able to stop and gawk like I wanted to because Melissa was hot on Gerald's heels as he walked us through his house towards the backyard.

Once we reached the pathway to the separated housing quarters, I realized we hadn't needed to go through the house at all to reach the property. Mr. Dawson had just wanted to impress us with the million-dollar décor of his house.

Rich people.

Melissa and I followed Gerald into the mother-in-law quarters, and at first glance, it looked palatial. It made me wonder who he planned on moving in here.

"So," he began, "as you can see, it has plenty of space and light. I dare say it's better than most average homes and I know you'll design it to match the splendor of the main house."

Again. Rich people.

Jesus, could he be any more pompous?

"Of course, I can, Gerald. However, if you want the décor to match that of the house, I'll have to have a tour of the main rooms."

I pull out my notebook to begin taking notes when Gerald responded with, "Whatever you need, Melissa. Perhaps while you're taking notes on the social rooms, Emily can take notes on the bedrooms and private baths."

It took all I had to keep taking notes and not point out how transparent he was. Hell, he probably didn't care that he was so obvious. Money wasn't the root of obnoxiousness; entitlement was. And it was very obvious that Gerald Dawson believed himself to be entitled, even to that of another man's wife.

Melissa spoke up. "What do you think, Emily?"

I smiled at Gerald first, and then looked over at Melissa. "You're the visionary, Melissa, and I'm the note taker. The fact that we're never confused about that is what makes us such a successful team."

Before either could respond, Melissa's phone started ringing with a signature ring tone that I knew was reserved for her elderly mother. Without bothering to even look at the phone, she turned to Gerald. "Sorry, Gerald, I have to take this call. The ringtone indicates an emergency."

He waved his hand her way. "Don't mind me, Melissa. Please, I insist you take care of whatever you need to handle."

"Thank you, Gerald," Melissa acquiesced. She walked outside to take the call and I secretly wanted to go out there with her. Gerald didn't make me uneasy in a threatening way, but he did in a slimy sort of way.

"So, Emily, you don't feel like going outside your comfort zone and seeing what you can do on your own?"

What a dick.

However, Melissa had been right. Gerald was not bad to look at. He stood at six-foot I'd say, and he had that classic prep boy look. He had dark blonde hair and the matching blue eyes. He had aristocratic facial features boasting of a perfect nose, thin lips, and a defined jawline.

He was wearing a suit, but you could tell he was in good shape for tipping fifty. Either that or the suit was so expensive that it made it look like he was in shape. I had no doubt he was constantly surrounded by women half his age. His looks and the size of his wallet made his age a non-issue.

My polite and professional smile stayed in place. "I'm quite happy with the role I'm in at Swan Interior Designs. It's not a matter of being scared to venture out of my comfort zone, Mr. Dawson, so much as that fact that I'm extremely happy where I am. I don't need to explore anything else." I prayed he was reading between my lines of between his lines.

He cocked his head at me as he leaned in, invading my space. "But just imagine all the new things you could be experiencing if you were to…uh, take a chance," he went on.

I didn't back up. I wasn't going to let him intimidate me. I stood my ground as I replied, "That would imply that I feel like I'm missing something, and I'm not, Mr. Dawson."

"Call me Gerald," he allowed.

"Thank you, but I prefer appropriate titles since I'm merely the assistant," I retorted, short of rolling my eyes at him.

"Something tells me that you're more than a mere assistant, Emily. I bet with the right incentive you'd love being on top," he cooed like only an entitled, arrogant bastard could.

I didn't care if my next words took feminism back fifty years. "I don't need to strive to be on top, Mr. Dawson. My husband is more than capable of taking care of me," I threw out.

Melissa strode back into the room before he could reply. "I'm terribly sorry, Gerald. Family emergency," she explained.

"Nonsense, Melissa. I was having a wonderful time getting to know Emily a little better," he replied.

"Well, why don't you lead the way, Gerald, so we can see what we're working with, and we can create your vision," Melissa suggested.

"Of course, just follow me, ladies,"

We followed behind him and explored the entire bottom floor and most of the upstairs rooms. I took note after note and barely kept myself from cringing at some of his suggestions. All of Melissa's creations swam in taste and elegance, but it was clear Gerald wanted the guest room to scream money, not comfort or class. However, the thing about Swan Interior Designs was that Melissa wasn't one to be bullied. If a client were steering towards crass and tacky, she'd suggest that they change their vision, or she would drop them and recommend them to another designing firm. She once told me that she would never endanger her brand for the brothel look.

An hour and a million notations later, we were back in Melissa's SUV, heading back to the office. We weren't ten feet away from the curb when Melissa said, "So, how badly did he come on to you?"

I let out a strangled breath. "It wasn't that bad," I told her honestly. "However, he really expected me to just pull my skirt up and bend over for him."

She laughed. "Yeah, that sounds like him. Most men who look like him and have his kind of deep pockets rarely get told no." Melissa looked over at me. "Say the word and I won't have you work on this with me. I can get Belinda to support this project."

I was already shaking my head. "No, Liss. He wasn't that bad, and I'm not going to let some rich playboy run me off a job just because he doesn't respect the sanctity of marriage."

Melissa laughed. "Okay, but the second he crosses the line, let me know, Em."

"I will," I agreed. "Still, I don't think he will. Something tells me that his ego is big enough to withstand my rejection." And it was true. Men like Gerald Dawson couldn't see past their own self-importance to recognize a genuine rejection when it's hitting them in the face.

I was pretty confident that, right now, he was convincing himself that if I weren't married, I'd be naked underneath him by the end of the week. Little did he know, trust fund babies didn't do it for me. Marcus coming home sweaty, dirty, and exerted was what did it for me.

Hell, Marcus in any fashion was the only thing that did it for me.

I could feel my face burn as I recalled all the things that I had said to him Sunday evening. I still couldn't believe I told him I had thought about double penetration. I mean, who the hell said that kind of stuff out loud? Who the hell *fantasized* about that kind of sex? We'd never even had anal sex, and here I was, asking him to fill me completely.

The only reason I'd been able to face him Monday morning was because he had seemed very turned on by the idea. When Marcus had taken us to the bedroom, he had thrown me on the bed and had made good on his promise. He had taken his time and had loved me leisurely and thoroughly. However, the thing about going slow and taking your time was that he'd been able to talk as he pleasured my body.

And, Sweet Jesus, did the man talk.

He had promised to do the most wicked things to me, and the dirtier the promise, the wetter I had become. I knew Marcus loved me, and I believed him when he said I was the best sex he's ever had, but I knew I wasn't the best *fuck* he's ever had, and I wanted to be.

Comparing our sex life now to what it has been in the past, I think our respectable approach to sex may have contributed to the demise of my self-esteem. Maybe Marcus never would have said those things about Stacy, and maybe I never would have felt threatened by them.

My feelings were still hurt, but I had decided to move past the hurt instead of fall victim to it. Our situation still wasn't ideal, but we'd been given an opportunity to fix it, and I was going to do my best. Marcus was a wonderful husband, and I was blessed to be able to love him.

"Why so quiet?" Melissa asked, snapping me out of my thoughts.

I decided to test the waters of risk. "I'm thinking of taking a long lunch on Friday and going to Marcus' office to surprise him," I told her.

She let out a whooping sound. "Oh, honey, if you're going to *'surprise'* Marcus for lunch, then I suggest you take all of Friday afternoon off." Melissa side-eyed me mischievously. "Something tells me Marcus is more than a two-pump chump."

I laughed at her crudeness. "So, then, is it alright if I take Friday afternoon off, Boss?"

Her face was split with the biggest grin. "Absolutely."

CHAPTER 15

Marcus ~

It was close to closing time, but it wouldn't have made a difference. I hadn't been able to concentrate all goddamn day.

Today was the day that Emily and Melissa were to meet with that weasel Dawson, and my mind had been drifting towards imagined scenarios about the meeting all fucking day.

It wasn't that I didn't trust Emily because I did. I was just still smarting over her dissatisfaction in bed, and it was fucking with my thoughts and emotions. Even though I knew-with all my soul-that Emily would never cheat on me, I couldn't help wondering if *she* wondered what other men could do for her. It was possible that a douchebag like Dawson might make her mind wander and I hated the idea of that possibility.

Suddenly, the realization slammed home and I knew exactly how she had felt when she had overhead me talking with Scott. I wanted to be everything to her, and the possibility that she may feel like someone else could give her something that I couldn't really had me on edge. Even if she never cheated, I wanted *all* of her with me in every aspect of our lives.

Plus, Dawson wasn't ugly.

And while I've been reaping the rewards of Emily opening up more in the bedroom, with every new revelation into her desires, the more I realized how much I've failed her.

When she had started throwing out all her curiosities at me on Sunday night, I had never been so turned on. Still, when she had started talking about double penetration, I had felt like I'd been in a whirlwind of uncertainty. Emily was the sweetest thing around. I would never have guessed that her desires ran into the taboo section of dirty.

However, I'd be lying if I said the idea of being able to do all those filthy things to her didn't make my dick hard as granite. The random memory of her face covered in white still flooded me with the urge to tug one out wherever I was.

There was light tap on the doorframe of my office. I never shut my door unless I was in a meeting or conference call. I wanted my employees to feel comfortable talking to me, so I stuck to an open-door policy. I looked up to see Mark with his head halfway in the door. "Hey, Mark. What's up?"

"Just letting you know I'm heading out and I think you're the last one left in the building, Boss," he said with a big smile on his face.

My brows furrowed. "But it's only-"

Mark laughed. "It's *only* past six, Marcus."

I turned my wrist, and sure enough, my watch showed it was closer to seven than six. "Shit."

Mark slapped the doorframe twice. "See ya, Marcus."

I threw a hand up haphazardly as I started gathering my shit together. All the files could stay where they were. I just needed to shut down my computer, then grab my phone and keys.

I needed to get home to Emily, so she could shut these thoughts of Dawson down.

The entire drive home, I kept telling myself how ridiculous I was being, but the pep talks weren't helping. At this point, the only thing that was going to help was when I hit the finish line of fulfilling every one of Emily's fantasies and curiosities.

I was so eager to get to Emily that I didn't even bother parking in the garage. I stopped in the driveway and practically ran through the front door. As I entered the house, my eyes searched the living room and kitchen for her. When I didn't see her, I hoped she hadn't stayed late at work. I had scrambled to get out of the office so fast that I hadn't even checked my phone to see if there were any messages from her. "Emily!" I called out.

"In here!" she hollered back from the bedroom.

I followed her voice and found her pulling out some clothes from the dresser. My dick instantly stiffened in my pants at the sight of Emily with a towel wrapped around her body and in her hair. With a t-shirt in one hand and shutting the drawer with the other, Emily looked over at me and smile. "Rough day at work?" she asked.

I shrugged and walked towards her. "Not rough, so much as I just lost track of time," I answered. "How about you? How was your meeting with Dawson?"

She rolled her eyes. "We got the account and it's actually to design the guesthouse you built."

I lifted a brow. "But?"

Emily let out a light laugh. "He's such a pompous twit."

I smiled down at her. "Yeah, his opulence is a bit much."

"I'm surprised he doesn't have a carpet made out of hundred-dollar bills," she teased.

I wrapped my arm around her and pulled forward until her body was flushed with mine. Emily blushed and it looked so sexy on her. I brought my hands around to rest on her hips. "Did he hit on you," I asked because I couldn't help myself.

"Marcus…"

"Did he, Chill?"

"He made some suggestive suggestions, but he didn't touch me or anything," she admitted.

My hands tightened and I couldn't stop the agitation that clawed at my insides. "What exactly did he say to you?"

She was still wearing only a towel, but she did her best to look stern. "It doesn't matter, Marcus. It was childish and is undeserving of any further thought."

"Let me be the judge of that. What did he say, Chill?" I asked again. I wanted to know if I needed to go knock the motherfucker out or not.

This time, she rolled her eyes *at* me. "He just made stupid comments about me going out on my own and trying new stuff. He said, he bet I'd do well at being my own boss and I seemed like the type of woman who would like to be on top," she finally divulged.

"I'm going to kill that sonofabitch," I bit out, pissed beyond all sense.

Emily dropped her shirt, then grabbing my face with both her hands, stared into my eyes. "Marcus, listen to me," she started. "I told him I didn't need to be on top because my husband was perfectly capable of taking care of me."

"Fuck that, Chill-"

"Marcus," she snapped, trying to command my attention, "he stopped his nonsense after I said that to him. It's not a big deal." Then she slayed me with her next words. "Now you're going to have to get over it because we commissioned this deal, and I will be working with Melissa on the guesthouse."

I pulled her hands from my face and held her wrists captive. "The hell you are, Chill. You're not going near that motherfucker again," I snapped back.

Emily wrenched her wrists from my hold and took a step back "It's not like he's the first man to ever make a pass at me, Marcus," she reminded me.

"No, but it's the first time a man's hit on you since you blurted out that our sex life sucked," I threw out, voicing my issues to all and sundry.

Her eyes widened and I could tell my words had hurt her feelings. I hadn't meant to throw her words back in her face, but just like my words had gutted her emotionally, her words had emasculated me. "That's not fair," she rushed out.

I took her face in my hands and pressed my forehead to hers. "I'm sorry, Chill," I apologized. "I'm so fucking sorry, baby. But these insecurities between us are driving me crazy."

"Mar-" I crashed my mouth to hers and cut off whatever she was about to say. I needed to feel her. I needed to cement who she belonged to.

I reached up and pulled the towel out of her hair and I thanked every deity in existence when Emily's delicate hands started tearing at my shirt. I pulled my lips from hers and worked in a frenzy to help her remove my clothes. I kicked off my work boots and toed off my socks as she pulled my shirt off my shoulders and went to work on my belt buckle.

Emily's eyes were on mine when she said, "Our sex life doesn't suck, Marcus." I hissed when she reached down inside my boxers and wrapped her hand around my cock. "It can't suck because this feeling, this heat, this craving I feel doesn't suck. My need for you feels magnificent."

It wasn't lost on me that she said *her need* for me was what made her feel magnificent, not that *I* made her feel that way. Still, that was okay because I was going to change that.

I pulled the towel from her body, then wrapped her hair in my fist, pushing her to her knees. "Suck my cock, Chill." I ordered. "Let me see those pretty, little lips of yours wrapped around my dick."

Emily wasted no time in complying and my dick was in her mouth before her knees had even hit the carpet. "Mmm…" she moaned around the hardness.

I dropped my head back, closed my eyes, and just lived in the sensation of Emily's wet mouth taking me in. With every thrust of my hips, she came back for more, and I knew it wasn't going to take much to make me explode down her throat.

However, that's not what I wanted.

This was going to be to please Emily and to ease my insecurities.

I looked back down, and Emily looked like she was getting high off having my cock crammed down her throat that it almost broke my heart to make her stop. Still, I did. "Get up, Chill," I said, pulling my dick out of her mouth.

She looked up at me dazed. "What's wrong?"

"Nothing, baby," I answered, pulling her up onto her feet. I took her face in my hands as I kicked off my jeans. "I just need to taste you, Emily." I could see the blush again and I leaned down to kiss her as I walked her back towards our bed.

Her arms came around my neck and her tongue danced with mine. She tasted like mint and forever, and I didn't stop kissing her until she was lying across our bed, my body covering hers.

I started trailing kisses down her neck, and the second I reached that delicate spot where her neck and shoulder met, I gathered a chunk of her flesh in between my teeth and bit down.

Hard.

Emily let out a curse and I started sucking the tissue into my mouth, determined to leave a mark of possessiveness. Her body was going to be riddled with them by the time I was done. If she was determined to work on this project, well, then, she was going to show up to work every morning too sore to walk and covered in my stamps of ownership. I did not give one fuck if that made me look insecure or juvenile, either.

I released her skin and pulled back to take a look at my handiwork. The mark looked so brutal that my dick could have broken concrete. "I'm going to leave marks all over your body, Chill," I promised.

Emily's voice sounded breathless and desperate when she asked, "Does that mean I can leave marks all over your body, too?" As soon as the words were out of her mouth, her voice changed to embarrassed and timid. "Never mind, I'm sorry. I know you don't like that."

God, I really was a fucking dick.

I remember back when I was trying to get Maxwell Construction off the ground, telling Emily not to leave any marks on me during sex because I had wanted to make sure I always looked professional. At the time, I had felt my request was legit, but once Maxwell Construction had started doing well, I never lifted the ban and told her it would be okay again.

So, if I was keeping score correctly, I let Emily pull away from me for the past two years without noticing. I had drunkenly gushed about an ex-girlfriend while she'd overheard. I put a limit on how she could touch me for the sake of professionalism. I stopped showing her any kind of affection and made her make do with mediocre fucking, at best. And my worst offense? I had made her feel optional.

My dick deflated quicker than a popped balloon.

I pushed off her and the mark I was so proud of before was now taunting me. It no longer felt like a sign of possessiveness. Now it felt like a lame attempt to prove how much I wanted her.

I sat up with my back to her and seriously considered going to sleep on the couch with only my regrets to keep me company. Her voice quickly brought me out of my dark thoughts. "Marcus, what's wrong?"

I didn't look at her when I asked, "Tell me the truth, Emily. All this new stuff…is it because it's really what you want and desire, or are you doing all of this because you think if you don't, I'll never be satisfied with you?"

I felt her hop off the bed and I watched as she gathered one of the discarded towels and wrapped it around her body. She stood before me, her hair a wet, tangled mess, and her eyes full of uncertainty. "I knew I should have kept my mouth shut," she whispered sadly as she shook her head.

"Emily-"

She squared her shoulders. "If you must know the truth, it's a combination of both," she admitted. "Hearing you talk about how enamored you were of Stacy clawed at my self-esteem and hurt my feelings. I had believed that being your wife made me special to you somehow, but it didn't. Your desire and love for another woman-"

I stood up, pissed. "I've never said I was in love with Stacy," I bit out.

Emily actually had the nerve to fling her hand in the air like my statement had no consequence to what she was saying. "As I was saying," she continued, "I feel like second best. Whether it's true or not doesn't change how I feel. You were gushing over a woman you hadn't been with in over fifteen *years*. So, I started some self-reflecting and I realized that my…uh, lack of honesty in the bedroom probably contributed to your fond memories of her. I thought maybe if I could trust that you wouldn't judge me for my desires, maybe you'd talk about me like that. But now I can see how stupid that was."

I stood naked in front of her with my hands on my hips. "Why is that stupid?"

She cocked her head at me. "Because the lust isn't real," she said, causing all the wind to be knocked out of me.

CHAPTER 16

Emily ~
Last night had been a disaster.

I was pulling up to the Maxwell Construction building because I couldn't stand it any longer. My original plan had been to surprise Marcus for lunch, then hopefully, spend the rest of the afternoon in bed, but that had been before that crap last night.

I had never seen Marcus so livid.

"What the fuck do you mean that the lust isn't real?!" *he roared in my face.*

I shrugged a shoulder. "*We're pretending. You're pretending to want me to desperation because you feel bad you hurt my feelings over Stacy, and I'm pretending to believe it could be real.*"

"Goddamn it, Emily!"

"*It's true,*" *I insisted.* "*We're doing all this stupid shit to* prove *something, not because we're attracted to each other on this kind of level. I mean, c'mon, Marcus. You know I'm speaking the truth. If you had never walked in on me telling the girls that our sex life was* fine, *kicking off this damn chain of events, we'd still be having regular sex, then rolling over to our side of the bed afterwards.*"

His hand snaked out, and gripping my arm, he yanked me forward. "*I've always been attracted to you on this level, I was just afraid to offend you. But believe me, if I had known you liked being fucked like a dirty slut, I would have cum on your face the first night you gave me your pussy.*"

And because he was making this seem like this was all my fault, I went in for the kill. "*Really? Well, then, tell me, Marcus, how many times did you pull out of me wishing that I was Stacy because you were missing out on so much dirty sex?*" *I spewed at him.*

I closed my eyes and dropped my head against the steering wheel. I'll never forget the look on his face when I had asked him that question. He looked like he had wanted to murder me. Instead, he had stormed out of the room and left me standing there in astonishment that we had let ourselves get to that point.

For the first time in over fifteen years, Marcus had slept in the spare bedroom, and he'd been out the door this morning before I had even gotten in the shower.

My stomach was a jumble mess of nerves and self-doubt, but I knew I couldn't sit in the parking lot forever. I didn't want to be afraid of Marcus. I didn't want to be afraid to talk to him. And because I sure as hell didn't want my marriage to end, I opened the door and hauled my ass out of my car.

Maxwell Construction was a four-story, blue and grey block building located just outside the commercial district of town. Because of all the materials that needed to be stored sometimes, Maxwell Construction couldn't be housed alongside basic commercial property.

I entered the building, and I was immediately greeted by Amelia, Maxwell Construction's receptionist. "Oh, Mrs. Maxwell, how lovely to see you," she welcomed me.

"Hi, Amelia, it's wonderful to see you. How have you been?" I asked, not sure if I was stalling or not.

"Oh, I'm doing well," she answered. "Would you like me to ring Marcus?"

"Oh...oh, please don't," I sputtered. "I was hoping to surprise him and maybe steal him away for the rest of the day."

Her kind smile grew wider. "Oh, how sweet," she gushed. "My lips are sealed."

"Thank you, Amelia," I told her as I adjusted the strap of my purse, hoping for some added bravery.

"Well, you know the way," she said, still smiling. I just nodded and headed towards the elevators, then hit the button for the fourth floor to take me to Marcus.

The building's make-up was comprised of the first floor that housed the reception area, two conference rooms, and a small breakroom. The second floor was occupied by two more conference rooms, a planning room, a materials room, and another breakroom. The third floor was a sea of offices and cubicles. It's where all the administration employees worked. The fourth floor held a small reception area, a conference room, three offices for Marcus' project engineer, his CFO, and his Human Resources manager. Marcus' office was located individually on the other side of the conference room, away from everyone else.

I'd never felt more grateful for the layout of the fourth floor as I did now. If shit went south, at least no one could hear us losing it.

When the elevator dinged and the doors swooshed open, I walked out and didn't see anyone. Normally, Lilly, upper management's administrative assistant, would be at her desk because she vetted anyone who walked out of the elevators, but she wasn't at her desk right now. It made me wonder if maybe Marcus was in an important meeting, and this was a bad idea.

I made my way down the hall and turned to the left towards Marcus' office. The carpet was plush, so all you could hear was the ringing of Lilly's desk phone in the background. It was so quiet that I felt like that idiot character in horror movies that always walked towards danger.

I was approaching Marcus' office when I heard voices through his opened office door, the first voice being that of my husband's. "So, you thought you'd just come by my place of work, and I'd fuck you during my lunch?"

"Oh, c'mon," replied a vaguely familiar female voice. "No one knows I'm here."

And just like in those horror movies, my legs kept walking towards a danger I didn't want to encounter. I stood paralyzed in the doorway as I took in the sight of Marcus' body towering over a woman I couldn't see. She stood facing him in front of his desk while he stood with his back to the door in front of her.

The picture looked…intimate.

"Malory-" he began just as I witnessed her hands climb up his arms.

I must have made a sound, though the action escaped me, because Marcus stepped away from her as his head twisted around and looked my way. I couldn't look at his face, so my gaze slid past him to a very satisfied-looking Malory. She was the woman who had been Becky's plus-one at the barbecue.

People often speculated and talked tough about what they would do if they were ever confronted with a cheating spouse, but the reality of it was so much different than the hypothetical situation you hoped to never find yourself in.

Marcus had asked me what I would do if I ever found out he cheated on me, and at the time, I had told him I would probably stay with him because I loved him more than I loved myself.

But now…

Now I realized that, while I still did love him more than I loved myself, I *did still* love myself, though.

Somewhere during my self-realization, Marcus had made his way over to me. "Emily," he said, his voice sounding desperate.

I snapped out of my Malory-induced trance and looked up at him and all I felt was soul crushing pain.

And finality.

I turned and carried myself down the hallway as fast as my legs would allow. "Emily!" I heard Marcus shout after me, but I kept going. I flew past a shocked-looking Lilly as I wrenched open the staircase door as Marcus' feet thundered behind me. "Goddam it, Emily! Stop!"

Later, I'll astonish myself with how I practically ran down four flights of steps without breaking my neck, but right now, I was flying down the stairs as if I were in the best shape of my life.

I slammed my palms against the emergency exit bar and the sunlight and fresh air gave me a false sense of escape. I was a handful of feet away from my car and freedom when my arm was encased in a hard, masculine grip. Marcus grabbed me and whirled me back towards him.

His chest was heaving, and his face was a mix of panic and fury. I struggled to break free of his hold, but his fingers were digging into my flesh so hard that I knew I was going to have bruises. "Goddamn it, Chill! Stop it!"

"Let me go!" I yelled back.

"Not on your life," he snarled. "That was not what it looked like up there."

I scoffed. I was so tired of competing for my own goddamn husband. "It's not?" I challenged. "So, Malory wasn't up in your office for a quick fuck?" I kept trying to break free, but he wasn't relenting.

"She was, but-"

"But fuck me for ruining your guys' little lunch date?" I finished for him.

He shook me. "No. Never, Emily," he insisted, his voice a dangerous hiss.

My eye caught a flurry of red behind Marcus, so I angled my head to see around him, and the woman in question was standing there, an obviously interested party. There was nothing like being humiliated in front of another woman to bring your claws out. "How long have you been fucking her, Marcus? Since the barbecue? Or did you guys meet before that and her going to the barbecue was just some sick, little game you guys concocted?"

Marcus' face took on a look so incensed that he looked like he might stroke out. "I am not fucking that woman, nor have I *ever* fucked her!"

"Then why did she have her hands on you?!" I shrieked, not caring that we were drawing a crowd. Amelia and a couple of men that I didn't recognize stood behind Malory now. However, I was beyond caring if I looked like a shrew. "If you're not fucking her, why didn't you call security or throw her the hell out of your office the second that she made it clear what she was here for?!"

He leaned down, piercing me with his glare. "Because I was hoping to avoid a scene!" he bellowed.

"Well, it's good to know that causing a scene is worth more than hurting my feelings. Or did you just prefer to embarrass me instead of her?" His hand kept tightening around my arm, and I feared he was going to actually cut off the circulation to my arm.

"Are you fucking kidding me?!" he yelled, shaking me again. "I don't give two fucks about that homewrecking bitch!"

Before I could respond, John Phillips rushed up next to us and tried to calm our storm. "Marcus. Emily, why don't-"

I turned my wrath on him because the pain was so deep and so big that it couldn't be contained. "Why don't what, John? You don't want the entire building to know what a dirty, no good, cheating bastard your boss is?' I accused.

"I've never fucking cheating on you!" Marcus boomed.

I was so done.

I had only one question for him, and his answer was going to be what could heal us or break us. "Why were you standing so close to her, Marcus? Why did you let her touch you?"

"Emily-"

"Answer the fucking question!" I screamed out like a lunatic.

"Because I didn't want anyone to overhear our conversation!" he yelled back.

Because he didn't want to cause a scene like he said? Or because he didn't want to get caught by someone overhearing their plans?

I went numb all over without the proof I needed behind his answer. In an instant, I went from heat-filled rage to ice-old numbness, and Marcus must have seen it in my face because he let go of my arm. *"Emily, please..."* I took a step back and stumbled. John's arms were there to catch me, but Marcus reached me first. *"Don't touch her!"* John threw his hands up in a surrender motion and took a few steps back.

I pulled myself out of Marcus' hold and did my best to smooth down my blouse and skirt. A bigger crowd had gathered, and I had decided that I was done humiliating myself in front of all of Marcus' employees and girlfriend. "I'm better than second choice," I told him, my voice strong in its resolve.

"Wh...Ch...*what?*"

I ignored him and marched to my car. I was pulling the door open when Marcus spun me around to face him again. "Get your hands off me," I instructed, all the while doing my best to hold his silver gaze.

"Emily, don't do this," he pleaded. "Please, for the love of God, please don't do this."

"Don't do what? Don't choose *me?*" I asked, heartbroken but strong. "I'm done not being good enough, and I'm so done with feeling guilty because I'm not."

Marcus' fist connected with window of the backseat of my car, and everyone could hear glass shattering all around. His voice was razor sharp when he said, "I admit I could have handle Malory's proposition better, but I am not sleeping with her. I have *never* cheated on you, Chill, and I never will," he stated again, but this time, his voice held a tinge of fear.

I was so hurt, and my battered self-esteem was so crippled, I ignored the look on his face and the sound of his voice. I held onto the last of my strength. "You know what, Marcus? I don't even care anymore. Sleep with who you want to. Fantasize about who you wish you could be with. Chase whoever you want to chase. I'm done completing for scraps."

"No!"

"I know I told you I was happy with whatever you gave me, but that was before I knew exactly all I was getting," I said, ignoring his outburst.

I slipped inside my car, and I thanked whatever had Marcus paralyzed, because I was able shut the door and turn on the ignition before he snapped out of his stupor. *"Emily!"*

I hit the gas and swung out of the parking lot in reverse. The tires hit the street and I was gone without a backward glance. I didn't need to give the crowd anymore of my dignity.

I didn't need to give Malory anymore satisfaction.

And I didn't need to give Marcus anymore of anything.

CHAPTER 17

Marcus ~

I stood there, not fully understanding what had just happened.

I felt like my chest was caving in and I couldn't catch a breath. However, what I felt more than anything else was fear.

A soul-consuming, deep, panicking fear.

Emily had just driven away from me after telling me that she was done me, and I wasn't sure we were in a place that was strong enough to withstand this fucked-up misunderstanding.

"Marcus," John muttered, his voice careful and hesitant. He sounded like he was talking to a wounded tiger and wasn't sure what my next move was going to be.

Rage like I had never experience before pulled me out of my disbelief, and when my eyes finally began to focus again, they locked onto the catalyst of this nightmare. I stormed over to Malory, and lawsuits and criminal charges be damned, I bored down on this repulsive excuse for a woman and very clearly said, "If my wife leaves me because of you, I will hunt you down and I will fucking *kill* you." Her eyes widen and she gasped in shock over my unchivalrous threat. "I don't care if you're a woman and I don't care if I spend the rest of my life in prison. If I don't have Emily, I don't have anything. That means my soul can rot in hell and my body can rot in prison for murdering you."

This time, Amelia piped up. I could feel her hand on my arm as she tried to bring me back from the brink of madness. "Marcus, it'll be fine. Emily is just upset," she said hopefully.

I ignored Amelia. Hell, I ignored all the spectators that had gathered around and ran my way back up to my office. I grabbed my phone, wallet, and keys and barely had enough sense to lock my office door behind me as I went home to talk to Emily.

I didn't think things could get any worse than last night's fight, but I was clearly wrong. Years of silent assumption had damaged Emily deeper than I had realized. She should have been able to walk into my office and laugh at Malory's pathetic attempt to seduce me. She should have been able to walk into my office confident, strong, and *secure* in the fact that I would never desire another woman. She should be able to tell people that she *knows* I'd never cheat on her, not that she *thinks* I wouldn't.

She obviously wasn't feeling that from me, though.

She'd seen Malory put her paws on me and had given up immediately.

Emily had seen another woman coming on to me, and instead of confidently putting Malory in her place because she was secure in our marriage, Emily had stepped back, believing that I was capable of having an affair.

I drove home wondering how the fuck I'd managed to do so much damage to my wife when I've spent every day of the last fifteen years living just for her. It boggled my mind.

I thought I'd been doing everything I was supposed to and all of it had been undone by my thoughtless ramblings about a fucking girl whose face I couldn't even really recall anymore. And I'd been honest when I had told Emily that I never loved Stacy. I hadn't. Stacy had been a whirlwind of sex that had lasted a few months and nothing more. Stacy had never been anything more than that.

The drive wasn't long enough for me to find the answers, but as long as Emily didn't leave me, I'd spend every second trying to find those goddamn answers.

Hell, who was I kidding? There was no way I would ever let Emily leave me.

I had no problem giving her time to simmer down, so we could talk and work this out, but she wasn't leaving me.

Ever.

Over my dead body, would I ever let my wife divorce me.

I whizzed through the house until I found her in our bedroom, an opened suitcase on the bed. The sight of her yanking clothes out of the drawer almost had my vision closing off. I stormed over to the suitcase and immediately started pulling her clothes out of it.

Emily eyed her clothes in my grip and her lips rolled in between her teeth like she was calling on everything holy to keep her calm. She stalked towards me and reached out to rip her clothes from my grasp. "You're out of your mind if you think I'm going to let you leave this house, Emily. And you're really fucked in the head if you think I'll ever let you leave *me*," I growled like a madman.

She smirked like she had some sort of secret weapon to use against me. "And your grand plan is to what? Handcuff me to the bed? Hold me hostage in a warehouse somewhere?" she taunted. "Because in the real world, Melissa would look for me the moment I didn't show up to work. In the real world, your business would go under if you spent all your time babysitting me."

I tugged on the articles of clothing that we were currently wrestling for, bringing her closer to me. "You think I give a shit about your job or Maxwell Construction?" I asked rhetorically. "Because I don't, Chill. I don't give a fuck about anything or anyone but you and the fucked-up state of our marriage."

"Don't be ridiculous," she snapped. "We would lose everything."

"Jesus Christ, Emily!" I yelled. "How many times do I have to tell you that all I care about is *you?!* As long as I have you, I don't give a damn if I'm broke, rich, dying, or healthy!"

She let go of her clothes and said, "I need some time, Mar-"

I dropped the clothing and took her face in my hands. "No, Chill. I'll give you anything else, but I can't give you time away from me," I said, cutting her off, not wanting to hear her say the words.

"Marcus, please," she begged as her green eyes started to leak big, fat, heartbreaking tears.

I stared into her eyes, pleading with her to see the truth in mine. "I can't, Em. There's no way I'm going to give you a chance to find out that you can live without me because I *cannot* live without you," I told her honestly.

Emily started sobbing and I gathered her up in my arms. "It all just hurts so much," she confessed. "I feel ugly and boring and *low*. I feel like every other woman on the planet has more to offer you." She was crying so hard that I was scared she was going to start to splinter in my arms. "If we're somewhere together and a woman walks by or talks to you, I worry myself sick wondering what you think of her," she continued, and her naked vulnerability almost dropped me to my knees. "I'm always scared that you might wake up one day and realize you can do so much better than me, and it's exhausting, Marcus."

"Jesus Christ, Emily-"

"I'm so damn exhausted," she sobbed again, and I didn't know how in the fuck to help her. I didn't know how to fix this. I didn't know how to make her not feel that way. My words weren't enough because my actions had said it all.

I had taken my wife for granted, and I had assumed she was happy and secure, but I never asked. I never asked her if there was anything she needed from me that I wasn't giving. I never asked her anything because she never complained about anything.

Whenever she had said she was feeling ugly or fat, I never asked her *why* she was feeling that way. I had always just told her that she was being silly because she was beautiful or told her she was crazy because she had a great figure. Whenever she had said she felt gross because she was on her period, I'd just rubbed her stomach to help relieve her cramping, but I never told her there was nothing gross about her. We've never had sex while she was bleeding, but I gave two fucks about Emily's period. I'd gladly fuck her and wash the sheets later.

I just never asked *where* her feelings and self-perception were coming from. I just always threw out some pacifying words, thinking it was enough to make her feel better.

God, I was such a fucking arrogant idiot.

And now my wife-my beautiful, sweet, loving wife-was falling apart in my arms.

I held her in my arms, then sat her on my lap as I took a seat on our bed. I stayed silent as she cried and cried. I knew enough to know that I couldn't solve all of Emily's self-esteem issues because, while I was arrogant, I wasn't arrogant enough to believe that they all stemmed from how I treated her. Looking back on it now, I remembered all the times she would make small, self-depreciating remarks about herself when we had first started dating. As I thought about it now, that might have been why I'd always taken the respectable approach to our sex life. I had wanted her to always feel like I was making love to her because I had wanted her to feel special.

The problem I faced now was that I was a man. We fixed shit. That was how we were geared. We saw a problem and our minds raced with how to fix it. However, I couldn't fix this. Emily's emotions weren't something that could be fixed. They needed to be healed and I couldn't do that without her help. She had to be willing to let go of our mistakes and believe me when I told her that everything I was doing now and everything I was going to do was all for her.

"Emily, I'm sorry," I said, the anguish evident in my voice. "I'm sorry I never saw any of this. I'm sorry I wasn't paying attention. *I'm so fucking sorry.*"

"I'm sorry I never told you," she whispered brokenly.

"Emily, I swear to you, there isn't anything going on between me and Malory." I prayed she believed me. "She and Becky had just come back from lunch, and instead of leaving, she snuck up to the fourth floor and Lilly hadn't been at her desk to stop her." I wanted to fault Lilly, but the woman had a right to take breaks and go to the restroom. "She found her way to my office, and I knew exactly what she was up to when she shut my office door behind her."

"But it was open when I got there," Emily pointed out and I thanked God that she still cared enough to listen.

"I know, baby. As soon as she shut the door, I stood up, then went over to open it again." I kissed the top her Emily's head and just prayed and prayed for salvation. "She offered herself and I told her no, I swear to God, Chill. The only reason I was standing so close in front of her was because I didn't want to cause an unnecessary scene. And I wasn't expecting her to actually try to touch me. You have to believe me that I would have stepped away from her if your gasp hadn't caught my attention first."

"And if the roles had been reversed?" she asked quietly.

I let out a humorless laugh. "I would have gotten arrested for murder, Chill." Still, I knew what she was hinting at. "But you're right. I should have just called security and never given her a chance to pitch her suggestions. I'm sorry I handled it badly, but that's all I'm guilty of, Emily. You have to believe me, baby."

I could feel all the strength leave her body in surrender, or defeat, I wasn't sure which. "I believe you, Marcus. I…I just…"

"You just what, Emily?" I needed her to talk to me. I needed to know what I was battling. I was up against the fight of my life, and I needed to know exactly what I was going toe-to-toe with.

"When I heard you guys and saw you looking so intimate, it was like all my fears proved true. All my insecurities and reservations exploded in technicolor inside my head," she explained. "It's silly and childish, but I want you to be faithful to me because you can't stand the thought of being with another woman, not because you're married to me and feel like you *have* to be faithful."

Christ, she was killing me.

"Emily, while I can appreciate the fact that a woman is attractive, to actually *want* to be with another woman is not possible. And I'm sorry for assuming that you knew that, when I tell you I love you, I mean I love *only* you. I want *only* you. I live for *only you.*"

"And when you get tired of having to reassure me all the time?"

I maneuvered her until she was straddling my lap and I could look at her face. Her arms came around my neck when my arms went around her waist, and all I could think about was that this was how we should always be. "Chill, if I do this like I'm supposed to, I won't have to be reassuring you all the time because you'll *know.* You'll *know* there's nothing and no one for me beyond you."

Her green eyes shifted, and her voice was hesitant when she said, "I feel loved, Marcus. I feel loved and I feel appreciated. I feel like a true contributing partner in this marriage, and I feel content with our relationship, overall. But…" She had to clear her throat a little. "I don't feel desired. I don't feel sexy or confident. I feel like a housewife and not at all like an assertive, sensual woman. That's what I'm missing," she confessed. She was looking directly into my eyes when she spilled her secrets, and I knew she really meant what she was saying.

"Tell me what you need from me, Chill. I'll do anything you want to make you see yourself through my eyes," I implored her. She let out a deep sigh and I was afraid she was giving up before even giving me the chance to try to give her what she needed. I squeezed her hips in my hands. "I'll do anything, Emily. Whatever you want, whatever you need…*I'll do it.*"

Her hands came away from the back of my neck and she brought them around to cradle my face. "Anything?" she asked.

My chest caved in desperation. "Anything, Emily. *Any-fucking-thing.*"

She had the saddest look on her face when she said, "I want you to show me what it's like to be everything you want in bed."

"Em-"

"Stop and listen, Marcus," she instructed, effectively stopping me. "Just please stop feeling defensive and immediately reacting. Just listen to me and try to absorb what I'm asking."

Emily was right. I wasn't listening. I was constantly on the cusp of refuting her concerns. I was always ready to tell her she was wrong to feel how she's feeling just because her view didn't agree with mine. She was trying to explain how she *thought* I felt about her, not how I actually did feel about her, but all I was hearing was how I was failing her. "I'm sorry, Chill. I'm listening now," I assured her.

She took another deep breath and started over. "I don't want you to think about what I want or what you think I'd like. I want you to show me what *you* crave and desire from me. Not from the women in your past, but what you truly like and want from me-*your wife*-in the bedroom."

I had no choice but to tell her the truth since she was being so honest. "Remember your concerns earlier? Well, what if what I want is too sick and twisted for you to like?"

She gifted me with the most beautiful smile. "That's impossible, Marcus. That's impossible because I'll love anything you to do me. I'll love it because it would be with *you.*"

CHAPTER 18

Emily ~
Since I was a female, that alone should say it all.

I walked in on another woman hitting on my too-hot-for-his-own-good-husband and I'd been attacked with so much self-doubt that I needed Marcus' untethered passion to bring me back to his side.

I meant what I had said. I felt Marcus' love, and I knew he was proud of me and all I did for our home and marriage, but I wanted to feel desired, too. My insecurities screamed out for that reassurance.

I could tell Marcus was trying to figure out how to approach my request and that was defeating the purpose. I wanted Marcus out of his mind with lust that he forgot I was a person with emotions and concerns and just took what he wanted from my body. "Marcus, if you don't think you can d-"

His arrogance smirked. "Oh, I know I can do everything you're asking. That's not the problem, Chill."

"What's the problem, then?"

"There's not a problem, so much as I have a concession if I do this," he said.

A concession?

"Uh, okay. What is it?" I asked, my stomach a sea of butterflies.

"If I give you this, you have to take it as the truth, Chill," he told me. "You have to go into this believing that what I'm giving you, and all the things I'm doing, are because that's what I like and it's everything I've ever wanted to do to you. *With you.* It's not fair to ask me for this if you're not going to accept it without reservation."

I thought about his words, and he was right. I needed to find a way to start believing him when he expressed how he felt, and I was hoping that this was a good start for that. "I promise to not overthink it, Marcus," I conceded. I mean, it was the right thing to do. Marcus let out a heavy breath and his silver gaze started darting all over my face. "What are you thinking?" I asked.

The corner of his mouth lifted in a half grin as he answered, "I'm wondering where to start." His face was full of wonder. He looked like a kid in a candy store who'd just been told that everything was free. "Jesus, Chill, the things I want to do to your body. The ways I want to mark you and tear into you." His wicked words were working my nipples and tempting my pussy. I honestly didn't know what I'd gotten myself into with my request, but I was eager to find out. I wanted to see Marcus uninhibited, and I wanted to feel unrestricted.

My skirt was already bunched up around my waist when Marcus had straddled me over his lap, so my thighs were already bare for him as his arms lowered and his hands found my skin. I could feel his dick hardening beneath me, and my mind wondered at all the possibilities. I ran my hands through the back of his hair and leaned forward, kissing him along his jawline. When my lips reached his ear, I whispered, "I won't say no to anything you want to do to me, Marcus. And I won't tell you to stop, no matter how questionable your actions are."

He pulled back to look at me and his smirk was cocky and challenging. "What if I told you I wanted to fuck you in the front yard for all the neighbors to see?"

Maybe I should have insisted on the single stipulation of not doing anything that would land us in jail, but I decided to play with him a little and compromise. "I'd say I wasn't sure about spending the night in jail for indecent acts in public. However, if you wanted to fuck me in the backyard or with the bedroom curtains open, I wouldn't mind."

His eyes widened in surprise, and I knew this could be the beginning of something fun and just for us. "You'd let me fuck you in public, Chill?" he asked, his voice low and rough.

"I really think I would," I answered honestly.

Marcus let out a growl and the next thing I knew, I was flipped over and tossed onto the bed. I looked up at my husband hovering over me and the look of pure want on his face was enough to make me flood my panties. "It's a good thing it's Friday, Chill, because I'm going to fuck you so hard and ruin your body from head to toe that you're going to need Saturday and Sunday to recover."

My body shivered at his threat-or promise-and I was ready to beg, but Marcus stopped all thought as his lips collided with mine. I opened up and eagerly invited his tongue to play, tease, and tantalize with mine. Marcus was a skilled kisser, and his lips never missed their target.

I ran my hands up his back to tangle in his hair as he braced himself on his right elbow and ran his left hand down my neck and over my collarbone until it cushioned my breast and his thumb started grazing the nipple. A moan escaped from behind my throat as I relished his touch.

He stopped kissing me and began a trail of wet kisses and licks down my neck. And when he reached the mark he left on me yesterday, he hissed against my skin, "I can't wait to fuck you up, Chill. I'm going to ruin your body and make you such a slave for my mouth, hands, and cock that you'll never think about leaving me again."

My heart tilted and my body began to hum with his intense promises. "God, I hope so, Marcus," I feverishly replied. My body jerked as I felt his teeth sink into the flesh of my shoulder and my legs opened wider as he began to suck the skin between his teeth. My hips started to undulate against the roughness of his jeans with my panties already soaked through.

When he was done leaving that mark, he pulled up, then scrambled back off the bed until he was standing over my lying, flushed body. With his eyes never leaving mine, he reached for the collar of his shirt and whipped it over his head, tossing it on the floor.

I stared transfixed. The sight of Marcus' without his shirt on always dried my mouth and made me speechless. He was just so damn hot with all that muscle and those tattoos that decorated his body. My eyes broke his gaze and wandered to his hands as he undid his belt and worked on removing the rest of his clothing. I silently watched the show, and when Marcus was finally completely naked, it was everything I could do not to hop off the bed and jump him.

"Like what you see, Em?"

The bastard.

He knew the answer to that. "Maybe," I teased.

He started stroking his cock and my mouth watered. "Come here, Emily," he instructed.

This time, I gave him a smirk of my own. "Where?"

Marcus growled. *He actually growled.* He looked down at the floor before him, and then back up at me. "Get down here on your knees and suck my dick before I force feed it to you," he demanded, and I swear to God, I almost came.

I felt all those giddy, nervous emotions I felt the first time I had ever slept with Marcus. I hadn't known what to expect then and I didn't know what to expect now, and the anticipation was turning me into a hungry slut for his cock. I slid perfectly off the bed until my knees hit the floor and Marcus' dick was in front of my face. I was so hot with greedy need that it was a miracle I wasn't drooling.

Or maybe I was.

At any rate, I reached for his cock and the soft, velvety heat felt delicious in my hand. My lips had barely closed around the thick head when I felt Marcus' hand tangle into the back of my hair and grab hold. I took him deep down my throat and started working the sensitive underside with my tongue while awaiting his instructions. I was committed to this being about him, and so far, I was loving the thrill of uncertainty.

"I love the way you suck my dick, Em," he gutted out as he started picking up the pace. "But I love choking you with my cock more, baby." This time, he started fucking my mouth instead of letting me suck his dick.

And, yes, there was a difference.

I placed my hands flat against his thighs and worked my lip, teeth, and mouth over his thick, hard cock. I've never been able to swallow Marcus' entire length, and I think he secretly loved that if his comment about loving to make me choke on it was any indication.

"Shit, Em...I'm going to cum if you keep doing that," he warned as if I had a problem with that. I didn't. I've always loved sucking Marcus' dick and I lived for that first squirt of release down my throat. It made me so wet to watch him watch me swallow his cum.

I continued to rest on my knees as Marcus glided his cock in and out of my mouth. It wasn't long before I felt the head of his dick swell as a sign of his impending orgasm. I started moaning louder, letting the vibrations hum over his skin and then I decided to be bold. I pull back, stuck out my tongue, and Marcus let out a deep rumble from his throat as he followed my lead.

He grabbed the base of his dick and started slapping it against my lips and tongue. I looked like a whore waiting for him to cum on my face. "I'm fucking cumming, Em," he burst out right before he shoved his dick back in my mouth and shot his load down my throat.

I swallowed every last drop, and I was still hungry for more.

I lifted my eyes and was shocked that Marcus was staring down at me with a look of uncontrolled lust on his face when he should be looking relaxed after that. "Stand up, Emily," he instructed harshly.

I stood up, and the second my feet found purchase on the carpet, Marcus pulled my body to his and started kissing my neck again. I let my head drop back, giving him better access to the sensitive skin, and just enjoyed the feel of his lips and hands on my body.

He kept kissing my neck and shoulders as he started removing my clothes. He ripped my blouse down the middle and the hiss of angry fabric was music to my ears. I could feel my blood rushing in my head and my body becoming alert with his touch.

God, how I missed this feeling.

Marcus' hands reached down and tore at my skirt with enough force to cause it to puddle at my feet. I had already kicked off my heels, and so that left me standing in only my bra and panties. I was anticipating Marcus ripping those off, too, but he didn't. Instead, he took a step back and let his gaze travel down and up my body. "Take the rest of it off for me, Em."

I kept my eyes locked to his as I reached around my back and unclasped my bra. My breasts instantly gave way from their weight, and I let the bra straps slide down my arms until the garment joined the puddle of clothes at my feet. Marcus let out a hiss and my nipples were immediately pebbled and ready for the taking.

"Now the panties, Em," Marcus prompted. "Show me that sweet pussy, baby."

I hooked my thumbs on the waistband of my lace panties and slid them down my legs. The panties barely cleared my feet when Marcus gathered me in his arms, his naked heat flushed up against mine.

I wrapped my arms around his neck and went in for a kiss. He sank into my embrace and kissed me back with the need that I craved. I felt his hands all over my body, from my back to my hips to my breasts to the outside of my thighs. However, when his one hand snaked around my back and the other drove downwards to play with my pussy, I tore my lips away from his and let out a heavy moan.

"You like that, Chill? You like when I finger fuck your tight snatch?" My stomach tumbled at the word snatch. Marcus' dirty talk has always been on this side of playful or risqué, but he's never talked to me like I was just a piece of ass. It gave me a tiny insight to just how much he's held back all these years. Plus, the fact that the word didn't offend me made me see how much I'd been holding back, too.

He inserted a second finger before I had a chance to answer him, and I had to grab his biceps to anchor myself against his assault. "Marcus," I whimpered.

"What, baby?" he teased. "You don't like hearing how wet your pussy is around my fingers?" His lips landed on my jaw, then danced their way to my ear where he preceded to get filthier. "Do you hear that, Chill? Do you hear the slick wetness of your pussy telling me how hot you are for my cock?"

I widened my stance and gave the only answer I could. "Yes."

His fingers worked their way in and out of my tight channel, occasionally swirling around my clit for good measure. Marcus plunged in another digit, and he was now stretching me with three long, thick fingers. They could never compare to the size of his dick, but they still made me feel full. "What would you do with four of my fingers shoved up your cunt, Em?"

My knees buckled and the arm he had around my back tightened, saving me from becoming a weak mess on the floor. Marcus has never tried to get four fingers inside me. I was a sputtering mess when I asked, "W…would…would a fourth one even fit?"

"I sure hope so," he answered. "Because the second your tight ass can take the pounding of my cock, I'm going to stuff your pussy full of every finger I can fit inside."

"Marcus," I cried out as I felt my pussy gush all over his hand, and I do mean *gush*.

He pulled his fingers out, then grabbing my hips, threw me onto the bed. I bounced twice, and when I looked up at him, his face was full of dirty intentions. "Spread your legs for me, Emily," he said, wasting no time. "Let those knees fall open so I can see that pretty little clit, that wet tight pussy, and your forbidden little starfish, baby."

My legs fell open and I pulled my knees up a bit so he could get a look at everything he asked for. "Like this?" I asked breathlessly.

His silver eyes dilated, and his jaw ticked. "Exactly like that," he said before hooking his hands around my thighs and pulling my body to the edge of the bed. This time, it was him on his knees before me and I laid back giving myself over to him freely.

I knew he was going to go down on me, even though I had told him this time was all about him. Still, I wasn't going to overthink it and I was going to trust him like he'd asked me to. I was going to trust that he was sticking his face in between my legs because *he* wanted to and nothing more.

I was going to finally let go.

CHAPTER 19

Marcus ~

My dick was rock fucking hard again, but it was going to have to wait.

Emily was going to sit back and welcome everything I've ever wanted to do to her, and I wanted to do so much more than just stab my cock into her pussy.

I've kissed Emily all over before. I've kneaded her tits and sucked on her nipples before. I've eaten her pussy before. I've fucked her missionary, doggy-style, her on top, spooned on our sides, up against the wall, and any number of other places outside the bed. So, a lot of what I planned to do to her wasn't new, but it was *how* I was going to do those things again that was going to be new. Now, while I enjoyed making love to my wife, I also appreciated a good, dirty fuck, and I've never done that with Emily.

I was going to do it tonight, though.

I was going to fuck her like a whore until she couldn't take anymore. I was going to push and push until I discovered her boundaries. And once I found those boundaries, I was going to spend the rest of my life playing inside of them. If she didn't want me calling her a dirty slut, I'd never say the words again. If she absolutely hated getting fucked in the ass, I'd never try it again. But if she liked the role playing and got wet at the words slut and whore, then I was going to whisper them in her ear when the occasion called for it. If she like getting ass fucked, then I was going to start playing with her ass more.

Right now, though, I was going to bury my face in her cunt and feast on her sweet body until she flowed freely all over my fucking face. I braced myself on my knees and I held her legs open with the weight of my forearms against the inside of her thighs. I brought my face up to her opening and inhaled.

As always, Emily smelled sweet and intoxicating.

I used my fingers to separate her wet pussy lips and took in all the cream that was soaking her slit. Even though she hadn't cum when I was finger fucking her, I had felt her wetness. She had been so wet that the slurping sounds of suction had been loud in my ears. I flicked my tongue against her clit, and the next thing I knew, her soft, delicate hands were fisted in my hair. "Marcus," she groaned as she opened her legs wider.

I pulled back and used my thumb to rub her hard nub, so that I could keep talking dirty to her. "You taste incredible, Emily. I love having the taste of your pussy on my tongue."

"Oh, God...yes...please," she yearned for more.

"Beg me for it, Emily," I told her, hoping she had it in her to play along. I knew the dirty shit coming out of my mouth was making her hot, but I wanted to see if she felt comfortable talking dirty, too. This was one of the boundaries I wanted to explore.

"Please, Marcus," she tried again.

"Please what, Chill?" I kept using my thumb to play with her clit while I pulled the words out of her.

"Oh, God," she moaned as her hands tightened in my hair. "Eat my pussy, Marcus. Please, lick me until I cum everywhere."

I almost came everywhere.

Jesus Christ.

Hearing Emily talk dirty was hotter than I thought it would be. Hearing such a sweet, reserved girl beg me to eat her pussy had me on the verge of cumming like a teenage boy.

However, since she did comply, I rewarded her. I stuck my face back in between her thighs and started swiping at her with my tongue while I pierced her gap with my middle finger, rubbing that rough spot right on the roof of her channel. *"Marcus..."* I wanted to fill her ears with the nastiest promises, but I was so entranced with her taste and the sounds escaping her lips that I chose to devour her instead.

I wanted to spend hours eating her out, but she was so worked up from the finger fucking I had given her earlier that it didn't take very long for body to start clenching around my finger. I licked, prodded, and invaded until her body bowed and she screamed out my name.

I removed my finger and replaced it with my tongue, letting her juices flood my tongue, mouth, and chin. My tongue was lodged inside her spasming pussy, and I kept flicking it, trying to gather as much of her cream as possible.

I wanted to drink from her.

I finally pulled away when her body started twitching at my contact. I knew she was beginning to feel the sensitivity from her release, so I wiped my face on her left thigh and crawled my way up her body, licking and nipping at her skin the entire way up.

Emily's eyes were closed, and she looked damn near catatonic that I wanted to pat myself on the back for a job well done. Then I wanted to kick my own ass when I realized how much I fucking missed this. While I've been eating her pussy and paying more attention to her body these past few weeks, I still couldn't believe I went over two years without going down on her and I didn't wonder about it.

I had let eating her pussy become optional. I had let a shitload of stuff we used to do become optional and I was so fucking sorry about it. Still, I did my best to push those thoughts aside. Right now, I needed to be here with her and not in our past.

I leaned down and kissed her, letting the taste of her sweet snatch touch her tongue. "See how good you taste, Chill."

"Mmm, Marcus...that was..." She didn't finish as she let her head just loll to the side. I used that opportunity to kiss the side of her face, down to her jaw, then back to her neck.

The more I touched and kissed her, the more I wanted to smash my head in with a bat.

I couldn't fucking believe I let us turn into roommates.

I was settled in between her legs and my cock was nestled up against her drenched center. "Emily, look at me," I bit out in regret and grief. Her eyes fluttered open, and the second I was sure she her green gaze was focused on my grey one, I viciously slammed into her body.

Her eyes squeezed shut and her nails raked down my back, trying to find some grip, and the pain of it made me violent. I wrapped one arm around her neck and gathered a chunk of her hair in my fist. I held myself up with other arm, and I started fucking her like my life was ending tomorrow. I pushed against her with so much force that the headboard was making dents in the wall.

I couldn't get deep enough.

I couldn't fuck her hard enough.

I searched her strained face and down to her bouncing tits. I felt like I was going to explode with all the things I was feeling. And that's when I finally understood why my words hadn't been enough to make her see how much I loved her. Words weren't enough because there weren't any words in existence that could describe what she made me feel. The only way she was going to see what she meant to me was for me to *show* her and never stop showing her.

Emily's eyes opened, and when she pierced me with her green gaze, they were filled with pure, unadulterated hunger and surrender. It sparked my dark, dirty side. "Do you feel how hard I'm fucking you, Em?"

She moaned, "Yes."

"This is how I'm going to fuck your sweet, virgin ass," I threatened, and she must have loved the idea because her pussy clamped down around me as she absorbed my words. I pounded into her as hard as I could and as deep as my dick would allow. "Tell me you want that, too, Em. Tell me you're going to endure all the pain it takes for me to be balls-deep in your ass."

She stayed true to her word about this being all about me. She backed up her request with determination. "Whatever you want, Marcus," she mewled. "I'll take whatever you want to give me."

Her eyes shut tightly, but I needed her focused. I needed her to hear and understand what I was asking of her. "Look at me, Chill," I ordered again. When she did, I let loose with the truth. "I want to fuck you like you're nothing but a dirty, easy whore. I want to call you names and just use the hell out of your body." Emily's eyes widened and I knew this was where my sweet wife would reappear and stop me.

But I was wrong.

Emily let out the sexiest whimper I've ever heard, and my cock hardened impossibly when she begged, "Do it." *Holy shit.* "I want to be your wife, your partner, your confidante, and your whore, Marcus."

I lost my mind.

I leaned down and bit her fucking jaw.

She screamed and I pulled out of her, then flipped her until she was on all fours.

I wanted to go slow. I had wanted all the necessities to take care of her after I fucked her in the ass. I had wanted to make anal sex as romantic and tender as I could. I had wanted her to enjoy the act so much that she'd let me keep fucking her there.

I had wanted to do a lot of things for her before introducing this into our bedroom. I had wanted it to be perfect and as painless as possible.

But fuck that plan now.

And I had warned her.

I shove my cock back into her pussy and held on to her hips as I bottomed out inside her cervix. It only took two seconds for me to find my rhythm and that's when I positioned my mouth over her ass and let a drop of spit fall, landing right on that fuckhole I've never breached.

Even though Emily was expecting it, she still tensed up when my finger started to make its way inside her ass. "I need you to relax, Em. I need you to push back, baby. Try to push me out, so when you relax, your body pulls me in," I instructed.

"Okay," she whispered as she did what I asked.

After a few pushes and pulls, I finally had my finger three knuckles deep in her ass. I dropped another bead of saliva over her puckered hole, and then really started to finger fuck her. *"Oh, Jesus Christ,"* she belted out.

I alternated invasions, my cock entering her pussy as my finger retreated from her ass and over again. I kept it up until I felt she could take another finger. Once I managed that, I started scissoring my digits, trying to work her open. "How's that for double penetration, Em?" I asked, remembering her curious fantasy. "Does it feel good, baby? Do you like have your pussy and ass filled up at the same time?"

She surprised me, yet again. "Oh, God…yes…Marcus…"

Thank fuck.

For me, it was a different sensation. I could feel my cock slide against my fingers through the thin membrane that separated her orifices. Plus, I was able to push down on my cock, guaranteeing that the head would rub up against her g-spot because I needed her to cum. I had no lube, and I had no plans to go easy on her. She wanted me to take her like I've always wanted, and I've always wanted to fuck her hard, deep, and rough in her ass.

I kept up the routine until those blessed words hit my eardrums. "Oh, God...Marcus, I'm going to cum..." Emily panted, very nearly there.

I started pumping my cock into her harder, then began to spread my fingers wider apart. I was going to slam my dick into her ass as soon as she coated my cock with her cream. "That's it, baby. Cum on my fucking cock like you came on my face."

"Marcus...oh, God..." she moaned, and her convulsions were all I needed.

I kept pumping into her, riding her through her orgasm, and the second I could feel her pulsing subside, I pulled my cock out, then worked the head inside her ass.

Emily was too wracked with the aftermath of her orgasm that her body didn't fight me, and I was able to pop through her tight, little ring with enough ease to not tear her. Once my cockhead breached her entrance, I slid inside in one smooth plunge, and I didn't stop until my balls were resting against her dripping, wet cunt.

"Are you okay, Chill?" I asked because...well, the fantasy of fucking her like a used-up whore was quite different from the reality of her being my sweet wife. I wanted to be rough with her, but I didn't want to seriously hurt her.

"Fabulous," she muttered out, lost in her own pleasure, and that was all I needed.

I grabbed her hips and started pumping into her ass like I've always dreamed, and she basked in the sensations like I'd always hoped, and the feeling was everything I knew it would be. Emily was hot and crushingly tight around my cock. It was all I could do not to cum after only a few pumps, but I held on. There was no way we were getting through this without Emily cumming again from this experience. She was going to enjoy this, even if it killed me.

After I established a rhythm and she was letting out moan after moan, I reached down and, with no grace whatsoever, I shoved three of my fingers inside her soaked pussy. "Oh, God...Oh, Marcus..."

"Take it, Emily," I grunted. "Take it all, baby. Take my fingers in your pussy and my cock up your ass." God, being able to say filthy things to her had blood rushing through my ears.

"I'm cumming, Marcus. Oh, God, I'm going to cum everywhere," she wailed.

I stuffed her as full as I could and as hard as I could. I fucked her for all I was worth and when both her tight channels clenched around my fingers and cock, I lost it.

I exploded deep in her ass as her pussy drenched my fingers, cock, and balls. *"Holy fuck, Emily."*

We came and came until we couldn't hold ourselves up anymore. We both collapsed on the bed, and I stayed locked inside her ass until my cock softened and eased out on its own.

I knew I should go get a washcloth and clean her up, but I just couldn't move. "Jesus Christ, Em, that was…" I couldn't find the words.

"I know," she whispered right before she said, "And I can't wait for you to do it again."

CHAPTER 20

Emily ~

"Hold up, wait a minute," Teri said, closing her eyes and shaking her head as if she heard me wrong. "Are you for real?"

I had called an emergency girls' night-well, afternoon-at Bransky's, a local bar because I had needed some advice and I knew the girls wouldn't hold back any punches.

Last night had been phenomenal.

Marcus had done things to my body I had never dreamed possible. The anal sex had been…well, it was one of those things that you had to experience to understand where the pleasure came from. And the double penetration? Jesus, that had been a slut-worthy moment.

It had felt decadent.

Afterwards, Marcus had carried me into the shower after he had regained his strength, explaining that he needed to clean us up because he'd read that it wasn't healthy to have vaginal sex after anal sex because of possible bacterial contamination if condoms weren't being used. And since he had plans to be in my pussy at least four more times, he had needed to wash up.

I had been stunned, and when I had pointed that out, he told me that he had read it somewhere. Then he had cradled my face in his hands and told me that he'd never had anal sex before, and so he had researched it online because he had wanted to make sure he made the experience as pleasurable as possible for the both of us.

I had cried.

I had cried because it *had* been perfect, and his words had made it special.

Marcus had spent the rest of the night adding things to our lovemaking that I had found erotic and exciting. He had slapped my ass, slid his cock between my tits as the head of his cock bumped my lips, smashed my face in the pillow, held me down against the mattress, and all kinds of other aggressive stuff that I never would have imagined. He had wrapped his hand around my throat and pulled my hair so hard that it had made my eyes water. He had called me a dirty slut and asked if I like being his whore when he had fucked me in my ass for a second time.

It had been dirty, filthy, demeaning, and, oh, so fucking hot.

He had made me feel like a goddess.

He had even managed to slip in small moments of tenderness, and it had thrilled me to still be able to feel connected to him as his wife at the same time he was calling me his whore. Maybe the secret was in realizing that everything was supposed to be an experiment in mutual pleasure. Just because I had let Marcus use me like a whore, didn't mean that he saw me as one. It was all role playing for the sake of hot, sweaty gratification. And while I knew me and Marcus were making progress, I was still confused.

Hence, the emergency girls' night/afternoon.

We were all sitting at a high-top table in the corner, away from random ears. I had just finished telling them everything from the night Marcus had overheard us to last night's argument. I even included last night's sex, but not the details. "Yep," I answered her.

"Wow, Em," Cynthia expressed right before she chugged what was left of her wine. "I had no idea."

"*We* had no idea," Jackie clarified. "I mean…I always thought things were sickeningly perfect between you and Marcus."

I took a sip of my beer before confessing, "It was, but then perfect turned into stale and boring."

Teri was leaning back in her chair with her arms crossed over her shoulders and I knew that wasn't a good sign. Teri was all about the truth, whether it was painful or not. She didn't overly care about the delivery. "Sooooo, let me get this straight," she started. "You overhear some drunk ramblings one night, and instead of confronting him, you went all passive-aggressive on him for two years, and then blamed him for the staleness of your marriage?"

"I didn't go all passive-aggressive on him," I denied weakly.

She scoffed. "The hell you didn't." Teri uncrossed her arms and leaned forward, her forearms resting on the table, her drink untouched. "He hurt your feelings, and instead of giving him a chance to apologize and make it right, you silently punished him to secretly get even."

"That's not true," I bit out as I slammed my beer on the table, Jackie and Cynthia quiet.

"Bullshit, Em," Teri continued. "Now, while I agree that he was a shit for not realizing he hasn't gone down on you for two years, this heartache is still all of *your* making."

"How is this all *my* fault?" I shrieked.

"Because you could have avoided all this had you not been too scared to either ask him to cum on your face or balls up and asked him what the fuck after you had overheard him," she explained simply.

I wasn't ready to accept all the blame. "So, Marcus is just an innocent bystander?"

"No," she quickly replied. "No, he's not. He should never have talked about another woman like that, and he never should have let you guys fall into a roommate stage, but he can't read minds, Emily. How the fuck was he supposed to know that shit had become stale and boring for you?" she asked.

I stubbornly took a sip of my beer without answering her. Instead, I said, "So, all my issues are unfounded, is that what you're saying?"

Teri let out a deep, regretful sigh. She never means to hurt anyone's feelings. It just happens with her lack of tact and logical approach to things. "No, Em," she answered. "But let me ask you this. Were you and Marcus having off the charts sex *before* you overheard him that night?"

I hated the answer. "No," I admitted.

"Then the stale and boredom had nothing to do with his drunken ramblings and everything to do with miscommunication on *your* part, right?" Teri sat back in her chair. "He's to blame for letting shit get stale, but *you're* to blame for not saying anything about it."

"She has a point," Jackie added.

Always the peacemaker, Cynthia piped up. "Emily, it's just…we've been with you for the entire duration of your relationship with Marcus and…"

"What?" I prompted.

"Well, Em…I don't think we've ever seen a day where Marcus didn't worship you," she said. "That man loves you to pieces, Emily. He might have been clueless, but he would never be unfaithful to you or admire another woman over you."

"She's right, Em," Cynthia agreed. "Marcus adores you. I've never seen anything else like it. Maybe he forgot how to show it, but that doesn't make his feelings about you unsure."

Teri leaned forward again. "Listen, Em. We're women, and for most of us, insecurities make up about seventy percent of our personalities, the other thirty is faking it. So, I get it. I really do. But you have one of the good one in Marcus, and you owe him an apology for handling the situation wrong, just like you expected an apology from him for handing the Malory situation wrong."

I shook my head in regret because they were right. "How did we get here?" I asked the air.

Jackie reached over and wrapped her hand around my forearm in a gesture of support. "You're not alone, Em. I don't know one married couple who hasn't neglected each other at some point or another. It happens to the best of us."

Cynthia added her point of view. "Sometimes we're so busy being mothers, caretakers, breadwinners, and whatever, that we lose sight of being wives. We tend to put our husbands on the backburner because we assume they're not going to go anywhere, and vice versa. It's not right, but it is what it is."

"So, did I fail?" I asked. "Is a marriage considered a failure if you let it get to the roommate stage?"

"No," Teri-the only person who's never been married-said. "Efforts only result in failure if you stop trying."

I chuckled. "So, I guess I owe Marcus an apology," I mumbled.

"You do," Teri agreed. "But don't forget, he owes you one, too."

Maybe they were right. Maybe we had already reached the roommate stage and that's why Marcus' words had affected me as deeply as they had. Maybe, subconsciously, I had already been feeling optional and it had been easier to play the martyr than to confront Marcus and find out that my fears had been warranted.

We remained quiet for a few minutes, and I figured Jackie and Cynthia were self-reflecting on their own marriages while Teri was probably debating starting her own advice blog.

After a few more minutes of silence, Jackie finally spoke. "So, the sex..."

I busted out laughing. "Yeah, the sex," I repeated.

"The best you've ever had?" Teri asked with a smirk.

I shrugged. "Well, Marcus was always the best I ever had," I clarified. "But last night was the best of the best I've ever had." Cynthia hooted and Jackie hollered. "And speaking of the best sex of our lives, how's the magnificent Christopher?" I asked Teri.

The smile on Teri's face said it all. "He's still magnificent," she answered as a blush swept across her face.

And Teri didn't blush.

Jackie placed her fist under her chin and leaned in. "Oh, really?"

"Did Teri tell you girls that she brought him to the Maxwell company barbecue, and he stole her away after being there for only an hour because he couldn't stand not being all over her any longer?" I ratted Teri out.

Cynthia and Jackie heads both swiveled in her direction. "Do tell," Cynthia encouraged.

Instead, I eyed Teri. "Admit it, Teri. You like Christopher for more than just a hot lay," I pushed.

She finally took a swig of her margarita on the rock before she answered, "Fine, I admit it. I like him for more than just a hot lay. There. I said it."

This time, the hootin' and hollerin' were blasted out by all three of us. "I knew it!"

"Relax, Em. It's not like you get a prize for this or anything," Teri teased.

"So, now what?" Jackie asked.

"Nothing," Teri shrugged. "We keep going until there's a ring on my finger or it fizzles out."

She was trying to sound casual about it, but this was anything but casual. Teri's been single and fancy-free her entire life. She's dated doctors, engineers, artists, and Taco Bell workers. The men in her life have been broke and wealthy, gorgeous and average, smart and simple. She liked variety and didn't have a preference. If she clicked with a man, she was game. If she didn't, she didn't waste her time. Plus, she's dated damn near every race that existed. She truly had no prejudices at all.

So, for her to admit liking Christopher…well, that was a big deal.

"He adores you, Teri," I said. "I see a ring before I see ashes."

"We'll see," she replied. "I mean-" Her phone rang, cutting her off. Jackie peeked over and started making the donut and hole gesture, letting us know it was Christopher.

Cynthia snatched the phone out of her hand and put it on speaker as Teri yelped in protest. "Hey, Christopher. This is Cynthia and you're on speaker," she warned him.

His deep, sensual chuckle echoed through the speaker. "Hello, ladies."

Jackie took over as she said, "Yeah, so, we're talking men, sex, and marriage over here and we were wondering what you got going with our friend, Teri, because she doesn't tell us shit."

"Ignore them," Teri shouted into the phone.

This time, Christopher let out an actual laugh. "Are you asking me what my intentions towards Teresa are?"

"Duh," I whined out.

Christopher was silent for a few heartbeats, and we all leaned forward towards the center of the table where the phone was, waiting for his answer. My eyes flickered up really quickly and Teri's intent concentration on the little device told me all I needed to know.

She more than liked him.

There was some clearing of the throat before Christopher finally spoke. "When I met Teri, all I wanted to do was sleep with her to the point where I ruined her for all other men. When I started sleeping with her, I realized I wanted to get to know her in between our sheet sessions. When I started getting to know her, I realized I liked what I was learning about her. I realized I liked *her*. However, what I became addicted to was how she made me feel every time I was near her, touching her, being inside her…even just how I felt when I was thinking of her." My body broke out in goose bumps at his open honesty. He could have told us it was none of our business, but because he knew how important we were to her, and she to us, he was putting himself out there. In my eyes, that said so much about him."

"And now," I asked, not being able to stand the suspense.

He chuckled again. "Now, I want to move her into my house and worship her every night God grants me on this earth."

Cynthia gasped.

Jackie was speechless.

I was melting.

And Teri…Teri's eyes became glassy.

"Wow," Jackie finally said, coming out of her shock.

And because he deserved it after putting his vulnerability out there, I asked, "Is there something you'd like to say to Christopher, Teresa?"

She glanced up at me and gave me a grateful smile. "Yeah, but I should probably say it to his face."

"If it's that you love me, you don't need to wait to say it to my face," he piped up through the phone.

She laughed through her happy tears. "I love you, Christopher," she finally admitted.

"Thank fuck, because I love you, too," he replied.

CHAPTER 21

Marcus ~
I had made it to the office before anyone else this morning because of a clusterfuck of a mix up on an environmental building we had contracted a few weeks ago. I had even had to go down to the site on Saturday to do an inventory of all the materials. The company was claiming to have ordered a hollowed block for the foundation base, but we had the order as solid block.

And I know we didn't fuck it up.

When dealing with expensive materials, we always tripled checked the request before ordering. Now, here I was, making sure all the paperwork was in order, so I could slap their environmental engineer in the face with it.

I had felt bad leaving Emily because, despite the mind-blowing sex we'd had the night before, I knew we still had a lot to talk about. However, she said that she had wanted to get together with the girls and me having to work gave her the perfect excuse to call them up and get drunk on a Saturday afternoon.

And drunk she had gotten.

When she had gotten home-tipsier than I had expected-she had raved on and on about Teri finally finding a good guy in Christopher, and then she had passed out before I could pick up where we had left off on Friday night.

I had made plans to talk a little more on Sunday, but apparently Teri's official relationship had been cause enough for a barbecue and party. So, we had gone over to Christopher's and had partied with the gang. It had been a great time, but by the time we had gotten home, it'd been too late for such a serious talk. I had buried my cock in Emily's pussy, and then we had fallen asleep in each other's arms afterwards.

I knew we were in a better place, but the unseen landmines still existed, and I wanted to snuff them out, once and for all.

I also needed to speak to my employees about what had gone down on Friday. I owed them an apology for the unprofessionalism and if it had caused anyone to feel uncomfortable, but I wasn't going to apologize for the fight.

Emily and our marriage came before anything and anyone else. I had meant what I said when I had threatened Malory. If I didn't have Emily, I gave a fuck about anything else.

I was knee-deep in order slips when Lilly poked her head into my office. "Good morning, Marcus. Uh…" Her hesitancy told me all I needed to know. The entire building must have heard about the fight by now.

I looked up at her and tried to put her at ease. "I need a meeting scheduled first thing this morning regarding Sampson Environmental. They're claiming we ordered the wrong materials and I need everything we have on their account," I said. I didn't bother telling Lilly who to call for the meeting because she's been with me long enough to know who should be included.

"Okay, no problem," she replied efficiently as she pulled out her little, handy, dandy notebook and started scribbling away.

I looked down at the watch on my wrist, and then look back up at her. "Also, I need a mandatory all-employee gathering at ten o'clock in Conference Room C." It was the largest of our conference rooms and the only one that could accommodate the entire building.

"Sure thing, Marcus," she replied again, scribbling like a maniac.

I gathered all the contract information I had with Sampson Environmental and headed towards Conference Room B. It wasn't ten minutes later that my senior project manager, sales manager, inventory manager, project supervisor, and contract manager started filing into the conference room.

I looked up once they were all seated and kicked the meeting off. "Tell me all I need to know, so that I can go tell Allen Stanley to go fuck himself," I demanded. It was almost an hour later before I had all I needed, so I could tell Mr. We're-The-Customer-You-Should-Be-Accommodating-Us-Stanley to go eat a dick.

Walking back into my office, I found Lilly placing a note on my desk. "Hey, Lilly."

She looked up. "Oh, hey. I was just leaving you a note. Everyone is convening to Conference Room C right now. You have about ten minutes," she said.

I nodded. "Thanks, Lilly. I'll be there in a bit."

Lilly passed me without another word, and for the first time since I started this company, I instructed her to close the door behind her. Her face was full of shock and wariness, but she silently nodded and did as I asked.

I just needed a minute.

I didn't have a speech prepared, and I just needed a moment to decide how I was going to approach this.

The man in me-*the husband*-in me wanted to just tell everyone that if they ever brought trouble to my doorstep again, they wouldn't live to regret it. However, that was a no-go for so many, many reasons.

The boss in me wanted to be professional and understanding *while* telling them that if they ever brought trouble to my doorstep again, they wouldn't live to regret it.

However, at the end of it all, no matter which way I went, they all needed to know that Emily came before them, this company, me…everything.

I finally made my way to the conference room, and it was packed. Apparently, when the topic was gossip related instead of work related, people couldn't wait to attend.

The murmurs died down as I approached the microphoned podium. I cleared my throat and scanned the sea of faces that made up my company. Everyone standing in this room has been loyal, efficient, hard-working, and dedicated to the success and growth of Maxwell Construction. It was the only reason I felt the need to apologize and touch on my personal life. They deserved an explanation, and they deserved an apology.

"Good morning," I opened. "I understand it's a Monday morning and you are all quite busy, so I'll make this as brief as possible." Once again, I scanned the faces and saw that they were focused on me with rapt attention.

I almost laughed.

"Some of you may have heard, and a few of you actually witnessed, an argument between me and my wife on Friday that I would like to apologize for." I paused and the silence was absolute. "I'm sorry for any concerns the argument may have caused. And I sincerely apologize for those who were subjected to any uncomfortableness that may have stemmed from witnessing the drama." I knew they wanted the details…I mean, who wouldn't? I just didn't know how much to say that would still preserve some privacy for Emily. I supposed the truth was still better than the exaggerated gossip that might be floating around, though. "I'm not sure what is being said, but the truth is-"

"It's none of our business, Marcus," Amelia interrupted with a sternness in her voice I've never heard before. "And no one should be gossiping about you or your wife."

I stared at her, absorbing her words, and that's when I realized that I needed to be completely honest with my team. "Thank you for that, Amelia. But that kind of compassion is the very reason that you all deserve an explanation," I told her with a smile.

I looked back at the crowd and said what I had to say. "My wife walked in on an employee's guest hitting on me and jumped to the wrong conclusion and became upset. And because my wife is my life, I chased her down and ignored all the rules of professionalism, and an argument broke out in front of the building." My eyes caught Becky's and she looked away. I wasn't sure if it was embarrassment or shame, but I didn't care. Her feelings were the least of my concerns. "As I go on, I want you all to, please, believe that I value each, and every one of you, and your contributions to the success of Maxwell Construction are unparalleled. However, as much as I value and respect each of you, not one person in this room is more important to me than my wife." I paused a second to let that statement sink in. "For me, Emily comes before anything or anyone on this planet. So, if it's a choice between Emily's happiness and anything else…well, Emily's happiness will always win."

Once again, Amelia piped up with, "As it should be, Marcus."

Her support was immensely appreciated. "For those of you who know Emily personally, I'd like to convey that she is fine-*we* are fine. But moving forward, the top floor elevator will now come equipped with scanned access and will be programmed into your employee badges. No unauthorized visitors or guests will be able to visit the executive floor without being escorted by a Maxwell Construction employee."

This time, it was Lilly who spoke up and addressed the crowd. "There will be a security company scheduled to come in this week to program the elevators and new ID badges will be distributed by the end of the week."

"Thank you, Lilly." She just nodded. "Thank you all for your time and understanding with this. That being said, I want you all to know and understand that, while I apologize for the drama, I don't apologize for putting my wife first. She will always be my first priority. Breathing, eating, and existing are a distance second while my family and friends come in third."

Amelia and Lilly started clapping with Lilly chanting, "Here, here."

"I think it's time to let you all go back to more important matters and, again, thank you for your time." I stepped down from the podium into the throng of employees and murmurs spreading throughout the room.

I felt a few claps on my back, and most everyone was smiling in support of my explanation, except for Becky. I wasn't sure if it was planned or if it was fate, but Kathy was standing next to Becky and I thought that was a good thing as I approached her and said, "Becky, I need you to accompany me and Kathy to her office, please." Kathy remained stoic while Becky's eyes started to gloss over, but her tears were nothing compared to Emily's.

We made our way to Kathy's office, and as soon as we were seated, I looked Becky in the face and explained how things were going to be from now on. "By the end of the day there will be a restraining order preventing Malory from stepping foot on these premises ever again. If you invite her here again, you will be immediately fired, Becky. Do you understand?"

She nodded. "I'm so-"

I held my hand up to stop her. I didn't want to hear her apologies, reasons, or explanations. "Also, I'm aware that you've been overheard having conversations about me on a personal level." Her eyes widened and her face flushed to a beet red, clearly embarrassed. "I need you to listen and actually hear what I am about to say, Becky." I gave her a second and she gave a small nod of her head. "I love my wife. I love her beyond human comprehension. If Emily asked me to slit my wrists because she was bored and needed to be entertained, I'd fucking do it." Becky gasped and that was just the reaction I wanted. I wanted this woman to *know* what Emily meant to me. "So, any ideas or fantasies about me need to come to an end. I will not allow your high school girl crush to taint what I have with my wife." Her tears finally started to fall, but again, I didn't care. "If you ever make another personal comment about me or my wife again, you will be fired on the spot. Do you understand me?"

"Y…yes, sir. I'm so sorry…" she sobbed.

"I don't need you to be sorry, Becky. I need you to show some respect and act professionally moving forward," I coldly explained.

She wiped at her face. "I understand, Mr. Maxwell."

I nodded and stood up. I faced Kathy and said, "Please write this up appropriately, Kathy."

"Of course, Marcus," she replied simply.

I walked out and headed back to my office wishing this day were over already.

I just wanted to be home with Emily.

She and Melissa were going to begin working on the Dawson account this week, and I knew the first week of a new project always ran her into overtime and she'd be coming home later than usual, and the thought depressed the fuck out of me.

It wasn't like I didn't have enough on my plate, especially with the Sampson fuck up, but none of it seemed to matter as much as being with Emily. I still felt like I was failing with her. It didn't matter how much I professed my love for her to the world. If she didn't see it or feel it, then my declarations were all for nothing. It didn't matter how great the sex was now if she still didn't *know* how I felt towards her.

I was always going to regret not paying attention. I was always going to regret how I had taken her for granted and had assumed that she'd been happy while I had never bothered to ask. And I'll never forget the look on her face and the sounds of her cries when she had confessed how seeing me with Malory had made her feel. The weight of her sorrow was like an anvil on my chest whenever I thought about it.

Fucking her into oblivion wasn't going to be enough. I just didn't know what more I could do. I've professed my love. I've worshipped her body from head to toe. I've apologized and have asked for forgiveness. I've threatened and begged. I just didn't know what else I could do at this point.

I shook my head and decided to table my personal issues for when I could actually do something about them. I wasn't sure what time Emily would be home tonight, but I knew we needed to talk soon. I couldn't take the uncertainty much longer. I knew we were safe from divorce, but I wanted more than that. I wanted Emily to be happy.

I wanted Emily to be happy with *me*.

I wanted Emily to be able to put in my eulogy that she felt blessed to be loved by.

I wanted her to be able to say that she knew *for a fact* that I loved her with all my being.

I wanted to be her fairytale.

I wanted to be her everything.

CHAPTER 22

Emily ~

Melissa let me take a long lunch on a Monday at the beginning of a new project and I couldn't thank her enough.

I had told her enough about how things hadn't panned out on Friday for me and there was no way that I'll ever forget what she said to me.

"Take a long lunch today and if you need to work a half day to make Friday happen, then just text me and let me know," Melissa said.

"But-"

She had taken my hands in hers and said, "Emily, listen to me. If your body is here, but your mind is on Marcus, for whatever reason, then you need to tell me, 'Melissa, I need a personal day to be with my husband'. End of story."

"But-"

"But nothing, Emily. Don't ever let anything come before what you feel for that man. Remember, there's a reason that in the event of an accident, it's your spouse who legally determines your life or death. He's that important. That means you should see him as such."

So, that's how I found myself back at Maxwell Construction, willing to face down everyone who saw me act a fool on Friday.

I walked in and immediately saw Amelia, and I was surprised to see the smile that radiated across her face when she saw me. "Emily, it's so good to see you," she beamed.

I smiled back. "Hi, Amelia, it's good to see you, too." I stepped to her desk. "Look, I wanted-"

She held her hand up to stop me. "It's good to see you, Emily. That's it. That's all, dear," she said so sincerely.

I was immensely grateful, but I still needed to take responsibility for my behavior on Friday. "Thank you, Amelia, but I would still like to apologize for how I behaved on Friday. It was-"

She stood up and leaned into me. "Emily, dear, you have nothing to apologize for. Had it been me, I would have bashed that tramp's head in with a stapler," she harrumphed.

I couldn't help but laugh. "I couldn't find a stapler," I teased.

"Well, you don't need one," she said cryptically.

"Uh, okay," I mumbled.

"I'll hold all of Marcus' calls and cancel his next two hours," she said with a wink.

"Thank you," I said, and then made my way to the elevator.

I couldn't believe how my stomach fluttered full of butterflies riding up the elevator. The weekend had been spectacular, and things were beginning to feel better between me and Marcus, so I wasn't sure why there were still pockets of apprehension.

Or maybe it was guilt.

The more I thought about what Teri had said, the more I realized she was right. I could have confronted Marcus the next day or even that night. I could have chosen to face the truth instead of shy away from an explanation. I had just been so scared that he had secretly been carrying a torch for Stacy all these years that I had chosen to voluntarily be second. And I had fed that choice day after day while accepting a position that Marcus never really put in me.

The elevator stopped and the doors swooshed open, snapping me out of my thoughts. I made my way towards Lilly, and she smiled at me, much like Amelia had, then waved me on through. I smiled back and kept walking. I felt like I should apologize to her, too, but if everyone was going on with their lives as if nothing untoward had happened, then I guess it was best if I just let things lie as they were. Besides, I didn't want to embarrass Marcus any more than I already had on Friday.

I still couldn't believe I told John that Marcus was a cheating bastard.

I definitely owed John an apology.

Suddenly, my thoughts paralyzed me in the middle of the hallway.

I owed *Marcus* an apology.

I had screamed and cursed at him. I had accused him of having an affair in front of the company he shed blood, sweat, and tears to create, and I hadn't once said I was sorry to him all weekend long.

And he never asked for an apology.

I had apologized for my breakdown, and I had apologized for my insecurities, but I never told him I was sorry for humiliating him in front of his employees.

The shame brought tears to my eyes and the realization of how unfair I have been to him all this time was enough to support my fears that I definitely was not good enough for him.

My feet started moving again, but this time, it was without fear of embarrassment. My purpose was to give Marcus the apology he deserved.

As always, his office door was open, so I walked right in. It wasn't until I shut the door behind me and turned the lock that Marcus' head shot up from whatever he was looking at on his desk. "Hey."

His brows shot up. "Hey." He searched my face, then asked, "Is everything okay?"

I folded my hands behind my back and leaned back against his office door. The tears came, but I didn't sweep them away. He deserved to see how sorry I was. "I'm sorry, Marcus."

He let out a sigh. "For what, Em?"

"I'm sorry I embarrassed you in front of all your employees Friday," I began. "I'm sorry for telling John you were cheating on me. I'm sorr-"

"Emily," he breathed out as he got up and walked his way towards me. Once he was standing in front of me, he lifted my face in his hands. "Emily, you have nothing to be sorry for."

I grabbed his wrists with both hands. "Yes, I do, Marcus."

"No, you don't, Em. I don't care what anyone thinks about Friday," he reiterated.

"But I was wrong," I implored. "I let them think you were a cheater and a horrible hus-"

"Do *you* think I cheated?" he asked, his silver eyes searching my gaze.

"No," I answered honestly. "Of course, not."

He let out a small laugh. "Then that's all I care about, Emily." His thumbs started swiping at my tears. "God, Em, your tears are like daggers to my soul. I *hate* seeing you unhappy."

"I'm not unhappy, Marcus. I'm just...I just feel like crap because you are truly the best person I know, and I painted you as some kind of asshole and-"

"Em, stop, baby. You're killing me," he interrupted.

I didn't know what to do since he wasn't letting me apologize. I wanted to let go of all my mistakes, but I didn't know how if he wouldn't let me apologize. "I don't know what to do," I whispered.

His eyes looked pained when he said, "Just let me love you, Chill. Just let me love you and love me back. And even if you don't love me back, I don't care as long as you never leave me." He closed his eyes and dropped his forehead against mine. "Sweet Jesus, just don't ever leave me, Emily."

"Look at me, Marcus." I waited until he opened his eyes and said, "I'm an emotional mess and I have a lot of issues I need to work through, but I love you. Through all the hurt, anger, confusion, and sadness, *I love you*. I've always loved you, Marcus. I will always love you. I-"

Marcus didn't let me finish. He crushed his lips to mine, and I kissed him back with so much regret and love that I felt like I would combust with what I felt for this man. I brought my arms around his neck, and he pushed me back against the wall with his body.

We kissed each other like we were never going to see each other again. It was frantic, desperate, passionate, and intense. It was everything I was feeling.

I could feel Marcus' hands reach down, then lift my skirt, and I wanted to weep. I wanted to cry with every hurt and every happiness he has ever made me feel. He started a trail of kisses across my jaw line, and closing my eyes, I let my head dropped back and just fell into the sensations he was making me feel.

"I've always wanted to fuck you in my office, Chill," he admitted heavily as his fingers found their destination.

A deep, desperate moan escaped my lips when he sunk a finger inside my pussy. I grabbed his biceps and held on as he started finger fucking me. "Yeah?"

His kisses turned into nips as he confirmed, "Yeah, I have." His other hand found my right breast, and soon, his fingers were pinching my hardened nub. "I dreamed of it, Em."

I opened my legs wider, welcoming the assault brought on by his fingers and made a confession of my own. "So have I, Marcus." He groaned, so I continued with my confession. "I've fantasized about surprising you naked. I…I've masturbated to fantasies of-"

He removed his hand from my breast, then brought it to my chin, forcing me to look at him. His eyes were dilated with lust and his finger was teasing just the right spot inside me. "Tell me what you think of when you're playing with your pussy, baby," he demanded.

I was already reaching my peak as he expertly played with me, so it was hard to get all the words out. "I've…*oh, God…*" I moaned.

"Tell me, Emily, or I'll stop," he threatened.

"I think about…about you making me suck your dick under your desk," I finally managed to get out. "I think about being bent over your desk."

"Jesus Christ," he growled as another finger joined the first and he started bringing me to the edge.

Through my haze of pleasure, I decided to give him what he wanted. "I always make myself cum at the thought of you fucking me so hard that everyone on the floor can hear me."

"*Fuck,*" he hissed.

My eyes fell closed, and I shattered around his fingers. "Marcus…oh, God…"

My body immediately felt empty as he removed his fingers from my core. I slumped against the door because I needed its support. I could feel the aftershocks of my orgasm and nothing else. It wasn't until I heard the tearing of fabric that I opened my eyes and looked down to see Marcus stroking his impossibly hard cock. His belt was hanging wide, and his pants were unzipped and opened. I had been so languished over the orgasm he had given me that I had missed him undressing.

Before I could utter a word, Marcus lifted me and had my legs wrapped around his waist. "I'm going to fuck you so hard and deep that all four floors are going to hear you cumming all over my cock," he swore right before bringing me down on his hard shaft.

Thank God I was wet with my earlier orgasm or else the pain would have been unimaginable. Marcus started pushing into me, and each thrust of his cock, slammed my back up against his office door. The wood rattled and thundered, and the vibrating sounds made me flood his cock. "Fuck me, Marcus," I begged. "Fuck me so hard that you have to carry me out of here."

"Jesus Christ," he cursed again as he picked up the pace and started really slamming into me.

The pain felt glorious, and the pleasure felt sublime.

Marcus was panting with his exertions, but that didn't stop him from adding my newest pleasure to the mix. "You want to be carried out of here?" he asked. "You want everyone to know you were in here getting your pussy fucked by your husband, is that it?"

"Yes!" I screamed out loud, not caring who heard.

Surprisingly, Marcus really got dirty and pushed me to the edge of my boundaries, even though we were in his office. "Beg for my cock, Emily," he commanded as he continued to pummel my body. "I want everyone in this building to hear you beg me to fuck you. I want you *screaming* what you want me to do to you."

I instinctively wanted to deny him, but he was helping me live out one of my dirtiest fantasies. It was one thing to emerge from the park bathrooms during a barbecue and have people *guessing* what we'd been up to, but it was something completely different to have people actually hear what we were doing. How embarrassing. How inappropriate. How *hot*.

However, when I remembered how I had made him look to everyone on Friday, any embarrassment I may feel at knowing that everyone would hear me was worth it if it absolved Marcus of any unfair judgments.

His fingers dug into my hips as he slammed harder and harder into my pussy, and I gave him what he asked for. "Fuck me, Marcus! Make me cum! Oh, God, please make me cum!" I screamed at the top of my lungs, giving into the fantasy.

"More," he snarled, and his demand brought on the telltale signs of another explosion.

"Yes, like that! Right there!" I yelled. "I'm going to cum, Marcus!"

The pictures on the wall started falling to the floor around us with the force of his thrusts, and the taboo, decadent thought that everyone knew what we were doing made me cum so hard that I was surprised the force of my convulsions didn't push Marcus out of my body.

"Fuck!" he roared right before emptying his cock inside me.

I must have passed out because, the next thing I knew, Marcus was whispering in my ear, "Chill? Baby, wake up?"

I pulled myself out of my exhausted haze and focused on his face. "Marcus?"

He chuckled as he pulled his dick out of my pussy and stood tall. He helped keep me steady on my feet until I felt strong enough to stand on my own. "You okay?"

I smiled up at him. "Never better," I answered.

He let out a full laugh then as he let go of my hips and started putting himself back together. Once he was done, he asked full of mischief, "Do you still want me to really carry you out of here?"

"Kind of." His brows raised. "I want you to call Lilly and tell her you're done for the day, and *then* carry me out of here," I clarified.

His smile made everything right in the world. "You got it."

CHAPTER 23

Marcus ~

I ended up carrying Emily out of my office, down the hallway, through the executive lobby, and into the elevator with the biggest smile on my face.

Emily's face had been buried in the crook of my neck, and I knew it was because, no matter how wanton she wanted to come across sexually, she was still shy, and her new sexual exploration was still all new to her. Plus, I knew her fantasies about exhibitionism were more wild thoughts than actually doing it.

Now, while I wasn't really much of an exhibitionist, Emily was my wife. What the fuck did I care if people knew that I fucked my wife? People *should* assume that I fuck her. And as far as making her beg me loud enough to bring the building down, that wasn't a power play or an attempt at showmanship. That was just another push at finding out just how far her boundaries extended and fulfilling one of her wants. Just like her admitting that she'd let me fuck her in the backyard or with the curtains open, I wanted to know if she wanted to experience people *hearing* us fuck as opposed to actually watching us in action.

I was a possessive man when it came to my wife, so I'd never let another man or woman see her naked. Still, I had no problem lifting her skirt and fucking her in public as long as all anyone could see was me owning her body and no one could actually *see* her body.

However, someone looking over and only being able to see me stand behind her, thrusting into her, completely covered by our clothing...yeah, I could handle that.

Once we made it out to the parking lot, I deposited her next to her car. "I'll follow behind you," I told her. I expected her to just nod. I hadn't anticipated her question, but, fuck, if it didn't make me hard again.

"What are you going to do to me once we get home?" she asked, her eyes full of lust.

"What do you want me to do to you?" I questioned back.

Emily's chest started heaving and it looked like whatever ideas were taking root inside her mind were driving her mad with desire. Her hands knotted in the front of my shirt, and it seemed as if she needed to contact to keep her grounded.

I felt like I was going to combust.

I wanted to fucking consume every single piece of her.

"I want you to use me," she hissed out, sounding desperate and wanting.

I stepped closer to her until she was trapped between the car door and my body. I wrapped my hand around her throat and squeezed. "Did everyone hearing you getting fucked turn you on?"

I could feel her throat swallowed around my hand. "Yes," she admitted.

"You want me to tell you how you're the best fuck I've ever had while I'm balls-deep in your ass?" I asked.

Her eyes flashed and I was surprised she didn't ask me to fuck her right here and now. "Yes," she forced out between the squeeze around her neck.

I leaned in closer. "You want to hear me tell you what a good, little slut you are for me?" *Fuck*. These questions were about to make me cum in my pants like a twelve-year-old first discovering his dick.

"Yes," she continued to admit.

"Say it, Emily. Tell me what you want," I insisted.

She looked so trusting when she said, "I want you to use me so badly that all that will be left of me when you're done will be my tears."

Jesus Fucking Christ.

My hand involuntarily squeezed tighter. "Why?"

"Because I don't want to be able to think," she answered. "I just want to feel you. I want you to make me *feel* your love for me." And then big, fat, heartbreaking tears started falling from her green eyes. "I want to *know*, Marcus. I want to know I'm taking you to places you've never been. I don't want to think it. I want to *believe* it."

I dropped my forehead to hers. "Promise me you'll forgive me when it's all said and done?" If Emily was truly serious, then I planned to use her to make every sexual fantasy *I've* ever had come true, and I wasn't going to stop until one of us was unconscious.

"Forgive you?"

The corner of my lip lifted in a smirk as I explained, "Emily, what you're asking of me is going to demand forgiveness later." I loosened the grip I had on her neck and ran my hand down her chest until I cradled one on of her large, heavy tits in my hand. "Because if that is truly what you want, then I'm going to commit the most depraved sexual acts against your delicious body."

Emily raised a brow and she looked fierce and confident, even through her tears. "You can do whatever you want to my body, Marcus. All I want in return is to be able to do whatever I want to yours," she announced.

My jaw clenched as I was hit with all the regret that I harbored over ever telling her not to mark me and making her feel like she needed to act accordingly. I keep telling her over and over that she owned me, but no wonder she didn't believe me. My *conditions* made me a liar. It's no wonder that she had kept all her sexual fantasies to herself.

I wouldn't have wanted to tell me, had I been her. It was easier to pretend that you could make do without certain things than to ask for them and be told no. And every stupid ass time I had put her desires on hold because I was a fucking idiot was like telling her no.

I really fucked this up.

I could only thank God that she was giving me another chance with her trust. This was my second chance to put substance behind all my claims.

"Em-"

Emily must have caught the instant tension because she started shaking her head. "I don't mean...I...I'm not going to mark y-"

"Fucking Christ, Emily, that's not what...I wasn't-"

Her face transformed from confident to so goddamn miserable that I almost dropped to my knees. And when she spoke, it was worse than being cut off at the knees. It was like she sliced my heart open and let it fall to the ground in pieces. "We're broken, aren't we?"

No, the fuck we weren't.

There was no way I'd let us be.

But I did know this wasn't the place to have this conversation. "Why don't we just get home, and we can talk there," I said, instead of denying or confirming her assumption.

Emily paled and started taking deep breaths. It was like she was steadying herself for the most horrible of news. "Okay," she whispered, nodding her head. "Okay, okay..." She started running her hand up and down her skirt and inhaling and exhaling like she couldn't control her breathing. "Okay..."

She was beginning to scare me.

"Emily," I snapped at her. "Look at me." She looked back up into my eyes and they were wide, fearful, and she looked just so fucking *lost*. "It's okay, baby. Everything is going to be okay, Emily."

I let out a sigh when a few seconds went by, and I realized she wasn't going to agree that everything was going to be okay. I reached around her, then opening the car door, helped guide her inside. She turned the ignition, then rolled down the window as the car came to life.

I leaned in. "Are you okay to drive?"

"Yeah," she answered so softly that it was a miracle I was able to hear her.

I didn't want to let her go, but I needed a few minutes away from her. Looking into her dejected face was making me lose my fucking mind and I needed to be focused if there was any hope of bringing her back to me. I stood up but was still looking down at her. "I'll be right behind you, Emily." She silently turned her head and started going through the motions of backing up and driving off. I stood there with my hands in my pockets watching her drive away.

I had no idea what I was going to say to her, and I had no plan, but I knew I had to do *something*. If not, her insecurities and my guilt were going to eat us alive.

After a few unproductive minutes of nothing, I got in my car, then drove home, praying that she wasn't giving up and packing her shit already. It was hard not to beat my head against the steering wheel during the drive home. I had never given much thought to the things I've said to Emily over the years because I never felt any cruelty towards her, so I never thought my words would ever be taken as hurtful.

It never, in a million years, occurred to me that telling her not to scratch me or give me hickeys early on would make her put restrictions on how she wanted to be with me. And I sure as fuck never thought that only making love to her would make her feel like she wasn't sexy. But then, I was a guy…love, attraction, sex, affection…it was all the same to me. It all revolved around Emily. How the fuck was I supposed to know that I had made her feel loved, but not desired?

I finally pulled into our driveway, and for a split second, I didn't want to get out of the car. I hadn't formed a plan yet. I didn't have the answer to make this shit all go away. I hadn't found the words to take back all the stupid, insensitive shit I've ever said.

I had Emily's love, and she's been handing over her body like a pro, but I didn't have her fucking trust, and I *needed* her trust.

It was imperative that I had her trust.

If she didn't trust me enough to hold all of the pieces of herself that she was offering, then what kind of husband did that make me?

It made me the kind of husband she was *settling* for because her dream guy wasn't me. The thought was like acid coursing through my veins as I finally got out of the car and headed inside.

I walked into the house to find Emily sitting on the couch. Her shoes were kicked off and her legs were curled beneath her with her head leaning against the backrest.

She looked defeated.

I sat down next to her and propped my elbows on my knees as I hung my head in my hands. Emily might look defeated, but I felt it.

Since I hadn't been able to find a solution during the short drive over, I said the only thing I could to her. "I'll do anything you ask of me in order to make this right, Em." I wasn't sure what I expected, but her next words sure the fuck wasn't it.

"I don't think there's anything you can do, Marcus," she replied. "I've been sitting here thinking and I think…I don't think *we're* broken. I think just *I* am."

My head snapped sideways as I looked at her. "You're not broken, Emily."

She nodded sadly, completely ignoring my words, and then it hit me. I was doing what I've always done. I told her she wasn't broken, demanding that she just believe me when I say it, instead of asking her why she felt that way.

I never *fucking asked her why* she was feeling how she felt.

I cleared my throat and *finally* fucking asked, "Why do you suppose you feel that way?"

"Because I can't find a way to believe what you say is the truth," she explained. "It's weird because I don't think you're a liar and I can't see you just actively lying to me just for sport. However, I don't believe you when you tell me that you're mine unconditionally. It's like my mind can't process it. So, something must be broken inside of me to keep me from trusting what you say."

Okay.

I could work with this-straight questions and straight answers. If we got the basics out of the way, maybe we could find our way through the rest. "Do you believe I'm faithful to you?"

"Yes," she answered immediately, and I was so fucking grateful for that.

"Have you always been faithful to me?"

"Of course, Marcus." Thank fuck for that answer or there's no telling what the fuck I would have done. Also, I knew Emily wasn't lying because, while she may question how I felt about her, I knew how she felt about me. I *knew* she loved me.

"Do you believe I'm happy being married to you?"

She hesitated a bit, but finally said, "Yes. I believe you're generally happy."

"Are you happy being married to me?" I asked, ignoring her hesitation.

"For the most part," she replied. "I mean, every day can't always be sunshine and rainbows, right?"

"Are you sexually satisfied," I asked, even though I knew the answer already, more or less.

"I wasn't," she answered honestly. "But I am now."

"Do you think I'm sexually satisfied?"

"No," she uttered sadly. "But I think we're making progress there, don't you?"

I nodded. "Yeah," I responded, not contradicting her. "However, I think that was just a lot of miscommunication on our parts. I think we'll be fine with that, eventually."

"I...I think that's possible," she replied simply.

And now for the emotional part of tonight's program. "Do you believe I love you?"

"Yes."

"Do you believe I'm *in* love with you?"

Her answer was delivered like a soft whisper, but the word shattered me like a motherfucking wrecking ball. "No," she answered.

I couldn't remember the last time I cried. I might have been a little boy, I wasn't sure. However, I could feel the burning behind my eyes as my wife-the woman I have worshipped for the past fifteen years-looked me in the face and told me she didn't believe I was in love with her.

The pain was incredibly overwhelming.

Still, instead of telling her that I was in love with her, I *asked* her, "Why do you think that?"

Tears were silently streaming down her face, but her voice was strong and sure and that scared the ever-lovin' crap out of me. "How can you be in love with a person you don't really know?"

CHAPTER 24

Emily ~

I was certain that the look on Marcus' face was going to stay with me forever.

He looked positively shattered.

Then he looked positively livid.

He stood up and kicked the coffee table over, and because that wasn't enough, he managed to lift it and hurl it a few feet away. "That's bullshit!" he thundered. His chest was heaving, and his eyes were on fire when he looked down at me. "I know you better than anyone else, Chill! Nobody fucking knows you like I do!"

I stood up to meet his wrath. "Then how come you didn't know that I was feeling like second best? Why didn't you know that I wasn't sexually satisfied? Why didn't you know that I felt disconnected from you? Why didn't you know that I cry a lot when you're not around?"

He was trying to rein in his rage, but his words were leaked with pure venom. "That's not fair, Emily! I didn't know any of those things because you never fucking *told* me!"

I wasn't trying to hurt him, but this marriage needed a deep cleansing. "You're right, I never told you, but you obviously didn't know me well enough to notice the difference in my demeanor after I overheard you that night. You went on with life as usual. If you really know me like you're claiming, you would have spotted the differences immediately and would have asked me what was going on, don't you think?"

"I did notice the differences, but it didn't occur to me that they were negative changes because I always assumed that if something was wrong with you, you'd fucking tell me!" he kept yelling. "I can't read your goddamn mind, Emily!"

"You don't have to read my mind, Marcus!" I yelled back. "All you had to do was pay attention!"

He threw his arms up. "So, because I failed to ask questions that I didn't know needed to be asked, you jump to the conclusion that I'm not in love with you?!" He started pacing and muttered into the air. "I'm losing my fucking mind. Jesus Christ, I'm going to lose my fucking mind."

"Marcus-"

He stopped pacing and faced me. "No, Emily. Just fucking no." I stopped talking. "Just like I don't get to tell you how you feel, you don't get to tell me how I feel." He stepped closer and loomed over me. "You don't get to tell me that I'm not in love with you. And you sure as fuck don't get to tell me that I don't know you, that I don't know who you are, because I do."

The gauntlet has clearly been thrown down. "Then who am ?"

"You're the girl who'd rather be happy than rich. You're the girl who'd rather be comfortable than dressed-up. You're the girl who'd rather have four loyal friends than a hundred fake ones. You're the girl who'd rather stay home, reading a book, than go on a shopping spree," he started spouting off.

"Those are things anyone who's known me for ten minutes can figure out, Marcus," I coldly pointed out.

When he responded to my callousness, I wasn't expecting him to be so deadly accurate. "Fine, I'll be glad to tell you who you are, Emily. You're the girl who's so scarred by the abandonment of her father and the criticism of her mother that you can't recognize real love when you've been waking up to it every morning for the past *twenty fucking years!*"

The shot was dead center, and I gasped and step back from its force.

As his words hit their mark, I realized I was right.

It *was* me who was broken.

Me, and me alone.

I wasn't sure what my face looked like, but Marcus paled and tried to back track. "Em…" He reached for me, but I flinched and drew back.

"Don't touch me," I begged. "Please, don't touch me." I just needed a second.

Marcus froze and we were both left standing there, not knowing what to do or say next.

I felt like I couldn't breathe. I felt like the smallest breath was going to cause me to explode in pain and regret. "I…uh…I…"

"Emily, look at me," Marcus said, his voice quiet and soft. It was almost as if he were trying to talk someone off a ledge. And maybe he was.

My eyes sought out his, but I couldn't focus. Everything was blurry and swimming around in patches of color. My mind was explaining to me that it was because I was crying, and that made sense. That made sense, and so I held on to that one thing…that one and only thing that was making sense.

And then his words started ping ponging around in my head and they wouldn't be silenced. They were demanding to be heard and understood.

"Emily, baby-"

I held my hand up to stop whatever Marcus was about to say. I still needed to process the words he had said. My brain didn't have room for more accusations, assumptions, or revelations.

It was finally starting to make sense of why I was all over the place with my thoughts and emotions. It was finally clear why I didn't trust him. If I didn't trust him, then I wouldn't crumble if he ever left me. Withholding my trust was my safety net should he ever walk away.

And what if he did walk away?

It would hurt. I'd be devastated.

But I wouldn't die.

I wouldn't stop living.

So, did this horrible, painful risk that I've carried around forever really exist?

The horrifying realization that it probably didn't was hitting me full force.

I wasn't sure how long I stood standing in shock, but I was suddenly snapped out of my battering thoughts when I felt Marcus' arms band around me. "Chill...baby, say something," he pleaded.

"I love you, Marcus." It was the only thing I could think of to say because my mind was still spinning.

"I know you do, Em." His arms tightened around me. "I know you do. I fucking *know* it without a doubt in my mind."

I nodded into his chest. "Good," I mumbled. "That's good, that's good. You...you should know that."

"Emily, you're scaring the fuck out of me," he whispered.

Hell, I was scaring the fuck out of myself.

How could I have been so wrong?

How could I have been so clueless?

Fear of abandonment was classic 101 pop psychology for any girl whose father had walked out on her. Sometimes, it wasn't that bad if the girl had a mother who was supportive and strong, and while my mother had done her best, she'd often been negative and very critical of me. When I'd been younger, her negativity had made quite an impact on my life.

The tears had subsided, and so I pulled back from Marcus and looked up at him. He met my gaze, and I could see the worry in his eyes. I could actually see the emotions swirling around in his grey depths and I was suddenly feeling so wretched for everything that I had put him through.

No, he wasn't innocent in all this confusion, but I was the one who should shoulder most of the blame. These were my issues, not his.

He was just the sorry bastard who had chosen to marry a damaged girl.

"I love you," I said again.

"I know you do, Chill," he simply responded, searching my eyes. He was probably searching for a sign that I hadn't lost my mind.

"And you love me," I stated confidently.

"Yes, I do," he confirmed just as confidently before he went on to say, "Emily, what I said-"

I stopped him. "It's okay, Marcus. It was just the truth," I assured him. "I can't be mad at you for telling the truth."

He sounded so sincere when he asked, "Christ, Em, what are we doing to each other?"

"Fucking shit up, I think."

He barked out a laugh. "Jesus, Em."

I smiled up at him, and then the severity of the past few weeks washed over me, and I couldn't stop the scratch in my voice. "I'm so sorry, Marcus. I'm so, so sorry for everything. I just-"

He dropped his forehead to mine. "I don't need you to be sorry, Chill. I need you to tell me that you don't really believe I'm not in love with you. I live to love you, so if you don't believe that I'm in love with you, then I don't know what I'm supposed to do with myself. How am I supposed to exist?"

The tears started, but with as much as I've been crying these past few weeks, it wasn't a big deal to me anymore. "I'm sorry I said I didn't believe you. I do believe you. I do." I took a steady breath. "I think I'm just a coward. I think it's just safer to believe to be happy with settling than to believe it's the real deal, and then having it all fall apart." I closed my eyes. "God, it sounds so stupid when I say it out loud."

Marcus' hands brushed my hair back from my face. "It doesn't sound stupid, Em. And you're not a coward. I understand why you might think that, but I don't think you're a coward. I think we just suck at communication."

"I…I'm going to try, Marcus," I promised. "I'm going to do my best to let go and believe in what you show me."

It wasn't like everything was going to suddenly be perfect now just because I've been hit over the head with the issues of my childhood. I knew that. It wasn't that simple.

It was never that simple.

Plus, I didn't want to boo-hoo over my issues because, let's face it, in the scheme of things, there were way worse things in the world than an absent father and a critical mother. I just supposed I never questioned how impacted I was by all of it. Maybe that's why I'd been all over the place with assumptions and accusations. I kept trying to pinpoint what to blame all of this on and I just couldn't. First, I had blamed what Marcus said about Stacy, then I had blamed our sex life, then I had blamed my confidence…looks like I should have paid a little more attention to *why* I was feeling what I was feeling instead of beating myself up with all the emotions I didn't have a solid explanation for.

Marcus leaned down and dropped a soft kiss on my lips. He righted himself up, then promised, "And I going to do my best to pay better attention, Chill. This isn't all on you, you know."

"Most of it is on me," I argued.

"Maybe," he conceded. "Still, there were some things I could have and should have done differently. And believe me when I tell you that I'll never make the mistake of taking your contentment for happiness again. Just because you're not complaining, doesn't mean I don't need to ask you if you're happy."

I sighed and pressed my face up against his chest again. "I hate that I made you feel as if I was unhappy. I wasn't. I'm not." I wrapped my arms him tighter. "I was…confused, I guess."

Marcus' arms lifted my body until I had to wrap my legs around him to hold steady, and I was instantly reminded that I didn't have any panties on. We were in the middle of the most important conversation of our marriage, so I really should have been focused. Instead, I was recalling how he'd torn my panties off in his office.

Marcus sat down and brought me down on top of him. I was straddling him, and if he was remembering that I had no underwear on, he wasn't showing it.

I held my hands loosely around his neck as his hands held my hips steady. His kind eyes were on mine when he said, "So, you'll make the effort to speak up more and I'll make the effort to listen better. That's where we start, Em."

"And now that…things have been pointed out, maybe I'll start paying more attention to my feelings, also," I added.

His stare was piercing when he spoke his next words. "As long as you know that I love and want only you, Emily. As long as you understand that we are not broken."

I leaned down and kiss him softly on the lips. "We're not broken," I repeated.

"And there's no one else, but you," he said, kissing me back. "There hasn't been anyone else since the moment I saw you, Emily. There'll never be anyone else."

"I know, Marcus," I whispered regretfully. "I'm sorry I let those thoughts creep into my head. Deep down, I know you love me and have always been faithful. I-"

"Emily, I don't want you to know it deep down. I want you to just *know* it," he interrupted. "That's the part that's killing me, Chill. That's the part I'm going to work on. That's the part I *need* to work on."

I believed him.

I believed that he was here with me and that he was all in.

"All you have to do is keep doing what you're doing, Marcus," I told him, hoping he took the hint.

The edge of his lip lifted, and he asked, "Oh, really? And what is that?"

I rubbed myself over his lap slowly. "Are you going to make me say it?" I asked coyly.

His hands ran down the top my thighs and back up to my hips. "Fuck, yeah, I'm going to make you say it," he answered. "You think I forgot you didn't have any panties on?"

"Marcus…"

This time when he ran his hands up my thighs, he did it underneath my skirt. The material bunched up around my hips, and when Marcus' eyes lowered, his eyes landed directly on my pussy.

My wet pussy.

Marcus' hands spanned my pelvic area. His thumbs dipped in, and he started rubbing and opening up my lower lips. I could hear the wetness around his machinations, and it sounded dirty.

It sounded pornographic.

It sounded like the beginning to an epic fuck.

CHAPTER 25

Marcus ~

I was staring down at Emily's pussy lips, spreading them wide with my thumbs, and her little clit kept peeking out every other movement or so. She looked like a horny slut with her legs spread open and her pussy on display.

I knew we still had a lot to work on regarding the emotional state of our marriage, but it wasn't going to be fixed overnight. We were going to have to take this one day at a time and recommit to no longer taking each other for granted. Still, that didn't mean our sexual relationship needed to suffer while we worked on the deeper things. Now that I knew how much of a freak my wife secretly was...well...

She had done her best to clean herself up before we had left my office earlier, but I could see her pussy was still wet with our earlier release. It made me think of something and I wasn't quite sure how I felt about it. I've never tasted my own cum before, but I was dying to taste her.

Fuck it.

"What would you think if I told you I wanted to lick your hot, little pussy clean, Em?"

Her eyes widened. "But y...you..."

I looked up at her and arched a brow. "Would you let me?"

"But, Marcus, you...there's some of your cum still..."

I chuckled over how she could say some of the filthiest things in the heat of the moment, but she blushed like a virgin when it was all conversation. "I know," I told her. "I'm not even completely sure how I feel about it, but I wanted to ask about *your* feelings on it."

Emily sounded absolute when she said, "I'll let you do whatever you want to me, Marcus. There's nothing you could suggest that I'd say no to."

My dick turned to steel underneath her. It felt thick, hard, and painful. It was dying to get inside her. "Take off your blouse, Emily." She had her shirt off before I even finished my sentence. "Next, take off your bra. Let me see

147

those big, heavy tits, baby." Emily reached around and unhooked the constricting garment and flung it onto the floor. I didn't want to quit playing with her pussy, so I leaned forward and drew one hardened nipple into my mouth.

"Mmm, Marcus…" I slid my right hand in between her opened thighs, then pushed two fingers into her sopping wet cunt. "Oh, God, yes…"

I let go of her nipple and looked up at her. Emily had her eyes closed and her head thrown back as she was riding my hand. She looked so fucking stunning that I immediately knew where I wanted to take this. "You like riding my fingers, baby?"

"Yes," she moaned.

"How about my cock, Em?" I asked. "You like riding my cock?"

She opened her eyes and looked down at me. "I love riding you, Marcus. I love how deep you get when I'm sitting on you."

I removed my fingers and went to work on unbuttoning my pants. Emily jumped off my lap and removed her skirt, so that she was standing before me completely naked. I took in her naked body as I started removing every stitch of clothing I had on. "Turn around and bend over, Emily," I instructed. "Bend over and run your fingers up and down your wet cunt." I encouraged her as she turned around. "Give me a show while I take my clothes off, Chill."

I stared transfixed as she did what I asked. She ran one dainty hand underneath her body and between her legs and she started rubbing herself up and down, occasionally slipping a finger into her opening. I could have cum without even touching my dick.

I was completely naked, and had kicked all our clothing aside, but I wasn't finished with watching Emily play with her pussy. She was the perfect picture of sexy, hot, and whorish.

She looked fucking perfect.

"Do you have any idea how unbelievable sexy you look as you stand there with your legs spread, showing me that sweet, wet pussy, Chill?"

"Marcus…" she whimpered pleadingly.

I started stroking my dick, and I would have been fine jacking off as she played with herself, but I knew she wanted to get fucked. I knew foreplay and teasing weren't going to be enough for her right now. Since I already decided how this was going to go, I went to push at those boundaries of hers that we were still exploring. "Emily?"

"Mmm…yeah?"

"Take those fingers that are playing with your pussy and get them nice and wet," I instructed.

"O…okay," she agreed breathlessly.

I kept stroking my dick as she started fingering her cunt with alternating fingers. Once I was satisfied that her fingers were wet enough, I pushed at her boundaries. "Now I want you to take those creamed-soaked fingers of yours and slide them into your ass, baby."

Her entire body froze, but I wasn't worried. If she wasn't grossed out by the idea of me tasting my own cum, I doubt if there was much that would stop her from continuing to explore her or my desires. "You want…"

"You heard me, Emily," I reprimand her. "I'm back here stroking my cock as I watch you and I want to watch you slide your fingers inside that tight ass of yours, baby." I decided to let her in on my plans. "I need you to loosen that perfect starburst of yours because you're going to ride my cock, but you're going to ride it with your ass as your ride my fingers with your pussy."

Emily didn't get that far.

Her knees collapsed at the picture I painted for her, and I had to jump up and gather her in my arms. We fell back onto the couch with her trembling legs on either side of my thighs and her head thrown back against my shoulder. "Marcus…"

I was swimming in pure amazement.

"Did you cum, Em?"

Her answer was a softly uttered, "Yes."

Holy shit.

Emily was so worked up that she had come from just a slew of dirty words and promises. "Tell me why," I demanded. "Tell me why you fucking came."

"Because I love it when you talk dirty to me," she partially answered.

I ran my hand down her stomach and dipped into her wet honey. "And what else, Em?"

"Because…"

I shoved three fingers inside her pussy and started pushing and pushing. "Because why?"

"Because…oh, God, Marcus…because I love the idea of you in…" I lowered my mouth to the slender slope of her shoulder and bit into her until I tasted blood. *"Marcus…oh, God…"*

I released her broken skin and said, "Because you love it when I fuck you up the ass, don't you, Emily? Say it," I demanded again. "Tell me how much you love having your ass stuff full of my cock."

Emily started rubbing back and forth across my lap and I knew the filth flying out of my mouth was driving her out of her mind. It took her a few seconds, but she finally complied. "I love it when you…I love it when you fuck my ass, Marcus."

I had to clench my teeth to keep from cumming. With my fingers in her pussy and blood dripping down her collarbone from my bite, it was a miracle I hadn't shot off like a thirteen-year-old boy. "You love it because, deep down, you love pretending to be my slut, huh, Em?" She didn't answer and I couldn't take it anymore. I knew she loved the smut talk, but I needed inside her. I grabbed her by her waist and stood her up before me. "Bend over again, Emily."

She did as she was told, and as soon as she bent over and presented me with the perfect access to her pussy and ass, I leaned forward and spit directly onto her tight, puckered hole. I took my fingers and mixed her cum with my spit, then massaged it around her ass until it looked ready. If Emily thought I was being dirty, she didn't say anything. She wasn't objecting to anything so far.

I laid myself back on the couch and told her, "Get on my dick, Em."

She erected her body, turned around, then climbed on. Emily supported her weight with one hand on my chest, and with her eyes never wavering from mine, she reached back, grabbed by dick, then slowly, ever so slowly, she worked my cock in her ass.

I had to grit my teeth and dig my hands into her hips to keep myself from slamming my cock up her channel. After what felt like a million years, the head of my dick finally popped through her tight ring and she was able to slide down, taking my dick inch by inch.

It felt like fucking Heaven.

I've gone my entire life having never experienced anal sex, but now that I have, now that I knew how good it felt, and now that I knew how much Emily loved it, I planned on fucking her up the ass often. However, no matter how phenomenal it felt, it still didn't compare to unloading inside her pussy.

The innate, animal desire to shoot my seed into her pussy was a *need*. Even if we weren't going to procreate, I still needed to cum in her cunt.

I waited patiently while she found her rhythm, and once she did, I let go of one of her hips and positioned my fingers to line up with her pussy.

"Oh, God. Marcus…Jesus Christ," she groaned.

I was looking up at my wife with her head thrown back, her eyes closed, and her spectacular rack thrust out as she rode my cock and fingers, and it took all I had not to blow. I wasn't sure how much longer I was going to last, so I needed to get her to her completion fast.

With her tight ass wrapped around my cock, my fingers able to feel the motions through the thing membrane that separated her fuckholes, I was on the verge of losing my fucking mind. It was hard to speak, what with me losing my sanity and all, but I needed Emily to cum. "Next time we do this, it's going to be in front of a mirror, Chill. I want you to see how fucking slutty you look taking my cock in your ass and my fingers in your pussy. Would you like that?"

Emily's body started squeezing and her rhythm picked up. "Yes…"

"You like being fucked like a whore, Em?" She just mewled. She couldn't speak and I loved it. I loved being able to drive her out of her goddamn mind. "Beg me to cum in your ass, Emily."

"Marcus…"

"Fucking say it, Em," I growled. "Beg me to cum in your fucking ass, baby."

"Oh, God, Marcus…please…please cum in my ass," she panted loudly.

I couldn't take it anymore. I removed my fingers from her pussy, grabbed onto both her hips, then plowed up into her ass. I kept thrusting up and down until I couldn't hold back any longer. "I'm cumming, Em."

"Marcus!" she screamed as her ass spasmed and convulsed around my dick. She kept screaming my name as I kept praising hers. It felt like our orgasms were never going to end.

When they finally did, Emily's body dropped over mine, and we laid there, sweaty and panting, as we came down off our high.

After a while, Emily's sweet voice broke the silence, "Marcus?"

My hands were rubbing up and down her back. "Yeah, baby?"

And then she flipped me the fuck out. "I don't want to take a shower just yet. Take me to bed and leave me soaked in your cum."

I was almost forty-years-old, but my dick was hard again with the thought of my wife requesting to be covered in my cum. So, I carried her to our bed, fucked her up the ass again, then let her pass out, leaking all over the bed like she had requested.

After Emily's breathing had evened out and I knew she was asleep, I got up, took a shower, and made a decision to commemorate our new beginning.

I called Isaac Spears, the man who I've been going to for all my tattoo art, and asked him if he could fit me in. He wasn't working today, but when I offered to pay triple, he said he'd meet me at his shop in fifteen minutes.

I left a note for Emily just in case she happened to wake up, but I was pretty confident she'd be out for a couple of hours or so. That was plenty of time for what I had in mind. An hour and a half later, I was walking back into our bedroom with a bandage taped across my clavicle.

At first, it had been an idea to help ease Emily's fears and insecurities, but as Isaac started etching Emily's name across my chest, I realized that I was doing this for me. I wasn't good with words, but I had promised her that I would listen better and do my best to show her.

Well, what better way to say it every day without having to actually say it?

I was taking off my clothes to climb back into bed with her when I heard her voice, "Marcus?"

I turned around, and the sight of her under the sheet, looking a mess, was beautiful. "Yeah, baby?"

Her eyes widened as she took in my bandage, snapping out of her sleepy state. "Marcus, what happened to your chest? Are you hurt?"

I waited until I was completely naked before making my way to the bed. Emily sat up, letting the sheet fall to the side, and I knelt before her between her opened legs. I placed my hands on her thighs and said, "Remove the bandage, Em."

She reached up and picked at the tape until she tenderly pulled back the gauze. She gasped and her eyes were filled with tears. "Marcus…"

"I'm going to do my best to never let a day go by where I don't tell you how much you mean to me, Emily. But, in the event that we get lost again with life, I hope this will say whatever I might forget to."

But I was never going to forget to.
Not ever again.

EPILOGUE

Marcus ~

So, now that you've had a front row seat to how I almost ruined my marriage, I wish I could tell you that everything is perfect now, but that'd be a lie.

Because it isn't.

It isn't perfect because life isn't perfect.

My company is still a priority and Emily's job is still demanding. There are still bills to pay, laundry to wash, grass to be mowed, dishes to be washed, and...well, you get the idea.

And even though we still fuck like we're auditioning for a porn studio, there are nights that we've gone to bed tired. There are evenings when we aren't able to eat dinner together and there have been mornings where I was out the door before she woke up.

However, while life around us hasn't been perfect and the world hasn't changed just to accommodate my love for my wife, Emily and I have made small changes.

Now, if we go to bed without having sex or not falling asleep together, Emily carves out some time to come to my office during her lunch hour, so I can bend her over my desk.

If we don't eat dinner together, we set our alarms to ensure that we eat breakfast together.

When time allows for it, we shower together, even if nothing sexual happens. Of course, most often than not, something sexual happens, but still.

If I annoy her, she tells me immediately and doesn't let it fester.

If she annoys me, I find the words to explain and not just dictate.

When Emily feels emotional, I listen and try not to take anything she says personally.

If I'm feeling emotional, I tell her with that same intent.

And if we fight, we fight unafraid, but respectfully. We are so cemented in our commitment to one another that no fight can break us up, no matter

153

what it's about. So, it actually makes me feel secure whenever Emily gets mad and picks a fight. It tells me that she's no longer scared of me ever leaving her.

And the sex?

Jesus, Mary, and Joseph, the sex.

I had praised Jesus the day Emily finally reached her limits, and I realized our boundaries were pretty much the same. The things I enjoy and get off on are in sync with her desires and it always makes for some explosive fucking.

Looking back, I will always regret letting our marriage become stale. The experience holds a lot of remorse for me because we didn't even have children to blame the distance on. We had just gotten comfortable. We had gotten comfortable like a worn-out pair of socks. Socks, so comfortable that you didn't even notice the holes in them.

That had been us.

A comfortable, holey pair of socks.

But we aren't that anymore.

For the past two years, I've been Marcus Maxwell, Emily Maxwell's husband, and she's been Emily Maxwell, Marcus' Maxwell's wife. And we were going to work on being that every day for the rest of our lives.

Now, while every marriage or relationship is different, I believe that everyone can make at least one small change to find their way back home. And make no mistake, your spouse should be your home.

While parents should do their best to raise their children right, don't forget that all children eventually turn eighteen and move on from their parents, and that circle of life leaves you back where you started.

It leaves you with your spouse.

Now, while I might not have all the answers, but I do know this much; I know that if you tell your wife that you love her more than anything, when she tells you that she's not feeling well, you cancel your golf game and stay home and take care of her. If you tell your wife that she's the most beautiful thing you've ever seen, you worship every inch of her, even the extra pounds. If you tell your wife that you can't live without her, then you don't ever do anything that might make that happen.

Say what you mean and mean what you say.

Never forget, whatever you don't do for your wife, another man will. And if he can, then you are failing. And that goes the same for women.

If you're afraid to be open and honest with your spouse, you need to ask yourself why and fix it.

Communication is the key, and it will always be the key.

And I will always be a lucky sonofabitch to have Emily.

The End.

PLAYLIST

Trials of the Heart – Nancy Shanks
Whatever It Takes – Lifehouse
Going Through the Motions – Aftershock
Love A Little Stronger – Diamond Rio
Wolves – Selena Gomez
As The Years Go By – Vanessa Williams

ABOUT THE AUTHOR

M.E. Clayton works full-time and writes as a hobby. She is an avid reader and, with much self-doubt, but more positive feedback and encouragement from her friends and family, she took a chance at writing, and the Seven Deadly Sins Series was born. Writing is a hobby she is now very passionate about. When she's not working, writing, or reading, she is spending time with her family or friends. If you care to learn more, you can read about her by visiting the following:

Smashwords Interview

Bookbub Author Page

Goodreads Author Page

OTHER BOOKS

The Seven Deadly Sins Series *(In Order)*
Catching Avery (Avery & Nicholas)
Chasing Quinn (Quinn & Chase)
Claiming Isabella (Isabella & Julian)
Conquering Kam (Kamala & Kane)
Capturing Happiness

The Enemy Duet *(In Order)*
In Enemy Territory (Fiona & Damien)
On Enemy Ground (Victoria & William)

The Enemy Series *(In Order)*
Facing the Enemy (Ramsey & Emerson)
Engaging the Enemy (Roselyn & Liam)
Battling the Enemy (Deke & Delaney)
Provoking the Enemy (Ava & Ace)
Loving the Enemy
Resurrecting the Enemy (Ramsey Jr. & Lake)

The Buchanan Brothers Series *(In Order)*
If You Could Only See (Mason & Shane)
If You Could Only Imagine (Aiden & Denise)
If You Could Only Feel (Gabriel & Justice)
If You Could Only Believe (Michael & Sophia)
If You Could Only Dream

The How To: Modern-Day Woman's Guide Series *(In Order)*
How to Stay Out of Prison (Lyrical & Nixon)
How to Keep Your Job (Alice & Lincoln)
How to Maintain Your Sanity (Rena & Jackson)

The Holy Trinity Series *(In Order)*
The Holy Ghost (Phoenix & Francesca)
The Son (Ciro & Roberta)
The Father (Luca & Remy)
The Redemption (Nico & Mia)
The Vatican (Francisco Phoenix Benetti & Luca Saveria Fiore)

The Blackstone Prep Academy Duet *(In Order)*
Reflections (Grace & Styx)
Mirrors (London & Sterling)

The Eastwood Series *(In Order)*
Samson (Samson & Mackenzie)
Ford (Ford & Amelia)
Raiden (Raiden & Charlie)
Duke (Duke & Willow)
Alistair (Alistair & Rory)

The Problem Series *(In Order)*
The Problem with Fire (Sayer & Monroe)
The Problem with Sports (Nathan & Andrea)
The Problem with Dating (Gideon & Echo)

The Pieces Series *(In Order)*
Our Broken Pieces (Mystic & Gage)
Our Cracked Pieces (Rowan & Lorcan)
Our Shattered Pieces (Molly & Grayson)

The Holy Trinity Duet *(In Order)*
The Bishop (Leonardo & Sienna)
The Cardinal (Salvatore & Blake)

The Holy Trinity Next Generation Series *(In Order)*
Vincent & Cira (Vincent Fiore & Cira Benetti)
Salvatore Jr. & Camilla (Salvatore Benetti Jr. & Camilla Mancini)
Emilio & Bianca (Emilio Benetti & Bianca Mancini)
Angelo & Georgia (Angelo Benetti & Georgia Mancini)
Dante & Malia (Dante Fiore & Malia Benetti)
Mattia & Remo (Mattia Mancini & Remo Vitale)

The Rýkr Duet *(In Order)*
Avalon (Avalon & Griffin)
Neve (Neve & Easton)

Standalone
Unintentional
Purgatory, Inc.
My Big, Huge Mistake
An Unexpected Life
The Heavier the Chains…
Real Shadows
You Again
Merry Christmas to Me
Dealing with the Devil